The Other Side of Power

by

M.G. Lambert

The Other Side of Power is a work of fiction. All names, characters, places, and incidents either are the product of the author's imagination or are used fictitiously. Any resemblance to actual persons, living or dead, or events, is entirely coincidental.

Published by Principio Books, LLC.
14525 SW Millikan Way, #75822
Beaverton, Oregon 97005
info@principiobooks.com
www.principiobooks.com
ISBN: 1629080101
ISBN-13: 978-1-62908-010-9

PRINCIPIO

About the Author

M.G. Lambert grew up and still lives in South Florida, the setting for *The Other Side of Power.*

The author was a public relations and editorial executive for a major U.S. airline for a number of years and was based in Miami.

Principio will publish other works by Lambert including *The Richest Woman in the World, The War is Over, The Children, Franchise,* and *Once a Pelican.*

A Tribute

This story grows out of the ongoing struggle of commercial aviation, particularly in the U.S.A., to make flying affordable, comfortable, somewhat glamorous, financially viable, and available to anyone.

The author is grateful to the men and women who head the airlines and serve millions of people day and night, the pioneers of flight from the Wright Brothers, Earhart, Lindberg, Sikorsky, Hughes to the modern giants in the airline industry, Juan Trippe, Harding Lawrence, and L.B. (Bud) Maytag.

They were all geniuses and because of them we know how to run an airline—and how to fly.

Chapter 1

Hank Mason sank into his big brown leather chair, rubbed a hand across his forehead and into his thick black hair and sighed. Then, reluctantly, he reached for his phone. "Whitefield, I hate like hell to call you again, but what's the word on the note for the 747s?"

"Well," Whitefield cleared his throat, "our lead banker, Kilpatrick, says he can see to an extension of the note for 60 days. Under the terms of our loan agreement on the planes, the banks could take possession or force a sale. The showdown can hurt our credit to the point we might never recover in the lending market." He paused. "I think we ought to sell the 747s before we are caught in the squeeze. I talked to our broker in New York, and he's got that buyer in the Middle East…"

"Goddamn it, I'm trying to save this airline, not sell it to a bunch of Arabs." Moving up to the edge of his chair, Mason felt the muscles of his stomach tense, and gnawing pangs of urgency ran all over his body—they were becoming a habit. Hank was getting damned tired of living with his nerves hanging out there raw, bleeding every other second.

"I am trying to save Airways, too, Hank. We can't meet that mega-million note and keep the whole management staff, pay bills, and keep reserves. By anybody's arithmetic, it cannot be done."

"I won't cut my managers, and I want to hold off on the sale of the big birds. What's the latest cash-flow picture?" Mason lighted a slim cigar, the phone resting between his ear and shoulder. He had to calm down, get hold again. After all, he was in command, the boss. The success or failure of his airline ultimately fell on him—he could not come apart now.

"The figures look good enough to keep the staff on for another month or so, but that would be it. If the strike ends in another two weeks, well, that's another story, isn't it? The New York banks might be persuaded to wait longer if they could see an end to the strike, Hank."

"We let the managers go as a last resort. Look, they've stuck by me through all of this. I've turned them into reservations agents, mechanics, plane washers, and cleaners. And they've all come through without any loud grumbling."

"You won't consider a staff just to answer phones, and another to do strictly routine maintenance of the planes? We could cut a couple of million that way. Immediately."

"I hear you talking, but no, Whitefield. Why do you have to always make so much goddamn sense? Shit, you know there's not a chance of this strike's ending right away, so we'll have to keep looking at the numbers every day. Bring the facts and figures in here, and we'll see what we can pay later." Slamming the phone down, Mason forced his chair away from the long oak table he used for a desk and stared out the wall-sized glass windows that overlooked the hangar complex of Airways International.

The neon signs that spelled out the name of his airline were coming alive as a pink twilight disappeared and the night moved in on South Florida International Airport, the nation's newest, most modern air travel and cargo center. People were still bewildered by its vastness and intricacies—passenger trams that ran by computer, monorails that whisked travelers in and out from Miami and Orlando and points in between, underground hotels, and shopping centers. Despite some kinks in the mechanisms, it was the kind of sophisticated operation that had to come if air transportation was to function at peak efficiency.

His thoughts wandering from his own personal dilemmas for a moment, Mason remembered his decision to move his airline's headquarters from Miami to this location. His board of directors had fought to keep the offices in the congested Miami area, but he had finally convinced them to let Airways buy 200 acres here in what was, five years ago, little more than rugged Florida brush land filled with pines and cabbage palms. When news came, three years ago, that the port authorities of the East Coast of Florida had decided to jointly build this airport, his board had given him a hero's party to celebrate his foresight. It was just good thinking, Mason reflected, to anticipate in which direction aviation had to grow.

Now, Airways was the only airline based right in the midst of one of the busiest airports in the world. The air complex was the crossroads of international travel and air cargo between the Americas and was gaining stature as an important intersection of air service linking coastal points of the United States with the capitals of Europe.

Turning suddenly from his successes back to his despair, Mason looked at the 727s and DC-10s that sat idled around the enormous cylinder of a hangar measuring the size of a football field in diameter and rising eight building stories high. These were just some of his 80-plane fleet. The other jets were scattered around Airways' 50 system cities, grounded indefinitely on airport ramps and aprons.

Airways' jets had made their last scheduled flights almost two months ago when 2,000 flight attendants had shut down the airline by what had grown into a bitter strike.

Mason's heart began to pound when he thought about what could happen to his airline if the strike dragged on. He could be forced to liquidate—bankruptcy was simply not out of the question these days as the ranks of his employees seemed to think. Clenching his fist, he struck his chair, sending it spinning on its base. "Goddamn!" he said aloud. How had this happened? Where had he taken a wrong turn? Almost 20 years in this business—since he was a kid—filled with wins, and now this huge sinker. Deep inside he was a frightened boy again, standing on a lonely hill in a small town in Pennsylvania. He wondered now, as he did then, where he was going. Even more important, where were all his people going? Even if they didn't know it, didn't believe it, he was responsible for them. He held many of their destinies in his hands. He stopped, questioning that thought. Somehow he had never considered himself in the role of protector, but the strike, this forced stopping in his life, had evoked in him a storehouse full of new thinking. He was often surprised now by his own psyche. Before, he had always been too busy to think this way, too preoccupied with making his airline happen.

When Mason heard Robert Whitefield knock, he was relieved of his thoughts and glad that the silence would be broken, that he would be talking, deciding, making plans, that he would not be alone for a while. "Door's open," he called out, still staring at the sign growing more distinct now as the night become ebony. He turned slowly to face Whitefield, his executive vice president, his right hand. "Sit down, Whitefield…"

Mason had not put on the lights in his office, but the hall light which spilled in revealed, instead of Whitefield, a woman holding a revolver. It was pointed at Mason.

"My God," Mason said.

"Don't move," the woman told him.

Mason's eyes stayed on the gun which began to waver in her hand. "Was this a dream?" he asked himself. Then a shock of reality bolted through his body, and he could almost feel the adrenaline spew through his veins.

The woman motioned him toward the windows with the gun as she came into the room. "I often wondered what you really looked like," she said, breaking the dead silence.

Mason backed up to the windows. His legs trembled.

"I don't know who you are, but you're making a terrible mistake."

"There's no mistake," she said, her voice cracking. "My husband's a mechanic here and he hasn't worked in almost two months, and I am dying of cancer, see. This strike is costing us everything we own. We've got five children to feed. You're the whole reason for this strike. You're rich, and you couldn't care less about poor people like us. You just care about your money…and the girls who work for you. Those poor, stupid girls."

Her voice sank at the end of her statement, and Mason hoped that meant she was weakening in her attempt to shoot him. "This is no way to solve a strike—with my blood. Sit down and we can talk about this. I can help you." Be calm, he told himself. She's scared as hell, too.

"The only way you can help is to settle the strike and get folks back to work. If you're dead, the strike will be ended. You're an evil force, Mr. Mason. A devil on earth. I truly believe that." The woman began to sob, and the gun seemed to be extended from her like a foreign object which somehow had taken possession of her.

Mason stood against the windows without moving. "Please, if you kill me, there won't be a sudden end to anything but my life. Let me have the gun," he said, moving toward her slowly. A well of strength building in him, he told himself he must take command. If he raced toward her, she might shoot out of fear. If he did not take her, she might kill him to satisfy a plot she had obviously staged with some care.

When the woman's eyes fell for a moment on the gun, Mason lunged for her, his hands gripping hers and finally seizing her weapon. They wrestled for a few seconds, falling, the intruder clawing at Mason in an attempt to retrieve her revolver. She pulled at his arm, jolting his hand, causing the gun to fire into the ceiling.

They lay together on the floor, the woman crying out as if she had been hit by the blast.

Mason clutched at her. "You're all right." He slid the gun in the outside, lower right pocket of his jacket, steadied the woman, and walked her to the sofa. He felt a cold sweat breaking out over his whole body. Then, a chill of gratefulness and relief swept over him. The woman kept crying and Mason was silent, waiting for a chance to talk with this stranger who had tried to kill him.

"Go ahead," she said, trying to get her breath between sobs, "call the police. I deserve to be locked up."

"I'm not going to call the police. Maybe you're right about me, but one thing is for damn sure. Killing me is not the answer to your problems. I can forget all this. I understand what you're going through, and I wish things were different for you. I wasn't always well off." He stopped. "God knows my family went hungry enough, but that's not important now…" Mason got up and walked to the table, turning on a light that cast a faint yellow glow over the room.

"I don't know what I'm doing any more. I don't have a long time to live on this earth," she said, burying her head in her hands.

Mason opened a cabinet, removed a small machine, and set it on the long table. Sitting down, he began to work at the machine, and when he had finished he handed a check to the woman. "This is as good as cash. The bank it's written on will cash it without any questions," he told her.

"This is for $15 thousand!"

"It's good. You'll have to endorse it, but don't worry; I didn't do this to find out who you are. There are less expensive ways of doing that. It may help you a little." Mason wondered, after he'd made the gesture, why he was paying the woman off. Was it for his life, because he felt empathy for this desperate human being, or did he believe he was the cause of the long strike, and this was a way of soothing his conscience? He could not find a clear-cut answer.

"But…" the woman started crying again.

"Just go now and don't do anything like this again." Mason did not watch the woman leave but when she had gone, he went to the door and double-locked it. Never had he even considered doing that before, in this office or in any office he had ever occupied. Crossing to the corner cabinet, he poured himself a glass of Scotch and then stared at the phone, wondering what was keeping White-field, trying to blot out the horror of what had happened minutes before.

Even after a few swallows of the whiskey, the incident began to bother him again. He saw the whole ordeal with clarity and in sequence. The woman's words rang in his head: "…you don't care about poor people like us. You just care about your money and the girls who work for you. Those poor, stupid girls."

So that was the common impression of him. People like this woman and her husband spent most of their lives involved in this airline he had built into one of the nation's top trunk carriers—and they apparently thought him some kind of viper.

Until this moment, until this homely woman spoke to him in this way, he had never fully imagined himself through their eyes. Had his escapades with his flight attendants clouded out everything good about him?

There was a pounding on his door, and Mason sprang to his feet to unlock it. "Whitefield?" he called out.

"Yes, yes, open up Hank," Whitefield shouted.

Robert Whitefield was a short man, thin and precise in dress. His head was bald, giving his appearance an added dimension of cleanliness and order. "What on earth? You never lock your door. Are you expecting the CIA?" With mercurial action, he opened a folder and removed several computer spread sheets, promptly placing them on Mason's table-desk and with pencil in hand began to point to rows of figures.

"Mason," he said, his dark eyes peering over the frame-less, octagonal glasses. "What is it? You look as though you've jogged around the entire airport landing field. Do you have a fever? Look at the perspiration under the arms of your jacket."

Hank raised an arm of his brown suede jacket and was surprised he had sweated through his shirt onto his outer clothing. "Somebody just tried to kill me. That's why I locked the door. She pointed a gun at me and intended to put a bullet through me. The gun's in my pocket." He patted the revolver, which he could feel against his hip as he did.

"My lord, Hank. This is terrible. What happened? How did you stop this woman?" Whitefield frowned as he moved the papers aside.

"She got nervous and I took a chance, got the gun away from her. There's some of the evidence…up there." They both looked up near the center of the ceiling where the bullet had left its charred marks.

"The woman is sick. Has cancer, she said. And financial problems brought on by the strike. She's married to a mechanic."

"You have an obligation to tell the police, Hank. She might try again or she might kill someone else."

"She's a woman with five children. She's terminally ill. How can I tell the police? The rest of her life wouldn't be worth living."

"How do you know she has five children? How do you know she is in fact married to a mechanic? She may be some psychotic running loose. The streets are full of them these days. This is extremely serious, Hank, and I do advise you to call the authorities. I am amazed our own guards did not stop her at the front door."

"She knew how to get up here without being seen by the guards. She must've used the executive elevator. The guards don't watch it all that closely now with the strike on…nobody's coming in here much. I'm sure she was legitimate."

"I still say she could try again. You must report this whole episode!"

"Just trust me. I want to drop the whole thing." Mason emptied his glass.

"You're simply going to forget it then?"

"Yes, and count myself lucky to be alive to tell you about it. Brandy or Scotch?" Mason motioned with his glass, holding it up.

"No, neither," Whitefield said, shaking his head. "You know, Hank, you amaze me. There is sometimes not a bit of logic in your brilliant head. I wonder how you made the airline what it is."

"I hire logic, Whitefield. I'm just an arrogant bastard with guts, somebody who takes chances. I've come near death many times, and this probably won't be the last time." Mason knew if he allowed himself to think about the future—and death at the hands of some disturbed soul—he would be scared as hell at this moment. He froze his thoughts, ignoring his imagination.

"You're not afraid?"

"I'm surprised, in a way, it hasn't happened like this before. You know, this woman made me realize I'm a vulture to some people out there."

"Well, you're kind of a saint to your managers, if that counts and I think it does. Well, do you feel like looking at these projections of cash flow? Thank heavens we're still collecting from the credit cards."

"I'll look." Mason bent his long, lean frame over the table as Whitefield moved his chair up, obviously readying to answer questions. As Mason scanned the sheets, finally zeroing in on the columns with his fingers, Whitefield eyed his every movement.

"Is there any news from the National Labor Relations Board on the strike, or from anybody?" Whitefield asked.

"No, I called earlier, nothing. Our attorneys in Washington say to expect no word till Friday. There may be a resumption of talks then in the capital between the girls and us. That's what the national mediator says. I'm not sure he knows what the hell's going on," Mason said.

"Well, when does Washington or anybody in Washington know what is actually going on?"

They looked at each other and laughed, and then the moment of shared humor revived Hank for a minute, making him return to a kind of normalcy.

"Look, Whitefield, this strike really isn't going to come close to ending until we admit this airline is coming damn close to collapsing or being bought out by somebody waiting to pick our carcass."

Mason felt a sharp pain in his left leg. The attacks often came when he was under stress. "It's just the leg. I'm not going to have a coronary or a stroke," he said before Whitefield could comment.

"Is there anything I can do?"

"Wish you could get me a new leg, but other than that, no."

In a few seconds the pain was gone, and Hank Mason was on his feet looking at the horizontal lines of figures and at the bottom lines of totals.

"There is always the sale leaseback with the insurance company, Hank, as an alternative. And with the insurance people and banks burned on real estate the way they have been in the last few years, I think they're being brave offering to buy our real estate here at the airport and lease it back to us. Forty million dollars is not a bad offer on this property," Whitefield said, looking over the sheets.

"Their risk isn't that great. Some airline would lease this space if we didn't. So I sign a lease for a rent I'm not sure I can pay. And if I pay for a while, it's with what, the $40 million they pay me—I'd need that to operate with, not hold for rent money. Meantime, this property in the inflated market climbs to $80 million, and they increase my rent with cost-of-living clauses or some kind of escalation demands along the way. No thanks."

"It's a possibility and it is one option we might not have a long time."

"It's blood money. And I need to forget that choice. It's a last resort."

"The board would buy it."

"Sometimes I think the board would buy shit if you bagged it, Whitefield. Look, it's just not a good solution."

"Then what is?" Whitefield sat back in his chair. He stared blankly at Hank.

"Settling the strike. Getting back to work. I think I'm going to talk to the flight attendants myself." The idea sprang from nowhere. He had never thought of that approach before, and his spontaneous ingenuity pleased him. Rearing back from the table, standing, Mason put his hands on his hips and nodded his head in agreement with himself.

"You'd be walking into a death trap. Well, it would be your own funeral. In your position as president of Airways, you simply can't do that. After all, that is why we have a National Labor Relations Board and labor attorneys and negotiators."

"Why do we? So they can drag out a strike and establish job security? They're doing no damn good. They've settled nothing.

I want to sit down with the head of the union and talk eyeball to eyeball."

"Our attorneys told you a long time ago it's not a good idea to get involved closely with union people. There are channels…"

Stalking around the room, Mason looked at the thick brown carpet of his office but was oblivious to it at the same time. "I built this place, this airline, with these two hands, Whitefield." He looked up. "And while that sounds like a lot of public relations crap, it is my blood that's in those planes and in this building and in that hangar. I can't let a bunch of half-assed lawyers and egomaniacs running the unions take it away from me and the rest of our employees!" That was the spirit, Mason told himself, that created Airways. Why hadn't he climbed to this altitude before in his thinking? Had he been so depressed by the strike, by the peripheral problems that went with the shutdown that his vision was cut off? Finally, he had perspective.

"Mason, you're a fine airline president, but you have little regard for the customs of law and labor and the negotiating process."

Mason's face flushed red and his eyes enlarged in rage. "I may not, but I know a damn sight more than the NLRB and my goddamn lawyers about getting to the heart of the trouble. Both sides are double-talking. At least I will not do that."

"Please, cool down, Hank. After what happened tonight you could have a heart attack. I suppose I will have that drink after all. I'll take a brandy."

Moving slowly to the cabinet, Mason poured a brandy snifter a quarter full of amber liquid.

"Here," he said. "I'm sorry I got mad. But this mess does have to end." There was a calm in his voice as he told himself he must retreat from an anger that could grip him and propel him toward disastrous behavior if not illness.

The agonizing memory of the plane crash in a bean field in Belle Glade, miles west of his office, flashed before him. If he hadn't stormed into a rage—and in his own cockpit at that—over being shortchanged by the owner of the field in dusting the crop, he would not have that limp and that knife-like pain in his leg today.

"What we must do now is decide where and how to get the money we need to carry on. If you know potential lenders, board members…" Whitefield said.

"No, I can't let myself get in hock with another lender and the board is out of the question. I could not ask a board member. They've all told me to let the 747s go. But I know that's a mistake. If we don't operate the big ones on the New York to Florida run and between Florida and Los Angeles, we may as well give the routes to the competition. Besides, one day we'll fill those planes on every flight and one day we'll need them for Europe."

"You can buy new ones then. I think the 747 Special Performance craft might work more efficiently for us. It carries 200 and that simply makes more sense today than trying to fill 350-plus seats in the planes we have now." He waited, his eyes glancing over his short, stubby hands. "You're the power, of course."

Mason ignored Whitefield's plug for the newer version of the 747. "I have one last place to turn for money. It wouldn't even be missed from that source. I've held off a long time…"

"You don't have that much in your personal bank accounts—not that I know of—and it's the worse kind of business to go dipping into your own personal treasury. You simply cannot justify it to the IRS that easily—you had better forget it."

"It's not my money I'm thinking about. And you're right. I haven't got that much. I'm afraid what I could raise in good old hard cash wouldn't get this airline through a few hours of operation."

"It's ironic, isn't it? If the rank and file knew how little you're really worth in cash, maybe they wouldn't see you as that villain you've been thinking you are tonight."

"The trouble is," Mason looked toward the airplanes, their metal bodies gleaming in the strong light which shot down from atop the hangar, "I'm not rich in terms of cash but I represent a lot of money to them. A few board members own a lot more stock than I do. How do I get that across to employees? That I am a salaried employee? And I can be fired and I don't have a grievance committee to cry to?" Mason felt humbled when he thought of how little money he could claim in his own right, but lack of money never bothered him before. After all, his goal in life was not money—it was to run an airline, to build a company of people with talent and dedication, to operate a line that would last and grow and become a leader in aviation. Money was way down on his list, but now he needed money more than he ever dreamed he would. Still, it was only a tool, a means.

"Employees don't read annual reports, Mason, even though they're sent to their homes at your request." Whitefield pulled off his glasses.

The Airways president looked over his mechanical flock just yards away from where he stood, then turned to find Whitefield studying him.

"How about dinner with us tonight?" Whitefield said.

"No, I'll get something later. I...I have a short trip to make. Thanks."

Whitefield did not ask where Mason was headed.

Chapter 2

Hank Mason slid into the scarred, black leather seat of his 1960 MGB, the shiny red metal of the long hood reflecting the silvery night lights of the airport roads that connected with I-95 north. He spun the car over cloverleafs, around bypasses and finally onto the open road—a giant necklace of light for as far as he could see ahead and behind in his mirror.

In the distance and west ran the monorail between Miami and Orlando, and he caught sight of the high, over-road tracks that looped around and through the airport complex. With the movement of his car and others and the monorail train that sped past them, he felt relieved from the burden of the strike, for an interval, from the memory of the woman who had threatened his life and from the pressure of his last, frantic plan to borrow several million dollars from Lenoir Mason, the wife he had not lived with for more than five years.

He did not want to ask Lenoir for funds, but he had decided she was the only person on earth who would lend his company the money without an involved series of questions and forms and high interest rates. If she said yes, her attorneys would draw up a simple loan agreement and that would be that. *If* she said yes. He could not count on that, and going to see her unexpectedly was a gamble with his chances and his emotions. Finding her in one of her exotic states had been shocking for him at times.

Hank liked the sea spray blowing on his face as he drove along South Ocean Boulevard in Palm Beach, a road of yesterday mansions that even many multi-millionaires today could not afford to keep. Of course, some could. Lenoir Donahue Mason could. The big house, created in the 1920's by the leading architect of his day, Addison Mizner, stood between the Atlantic Ocean to the east and Lake Worth to the west. Both waters were hidden from view by masses of tropical foliage, palm trees, wiry purple and salmon bougainvillea, giant draping ferns, and plants Mason had never known by name.

The grounds surrounding the pink stucco house smelled of fresh-cut grass and night-blooming jasmine—Lenoir's favorite flower—and the salt from the sea. As he drove slowly through the lighted gardens, he heard the crunch of the small, sand-colored rocks under his car, and he recalled it was on a night like this that he and Lenoir had landed in Honolulu on their wedding trip 20 years ago. They were mere children then, so innocent and vulnerable.

The amber light that hung in the wrought iron fixture over the entranceway to the house reminded him of the torches the hotel keepers in Honolulu lighted just for them, outside their cottage, every night for the three weeks they stayed in the islands.

After letting himself in with his key, Mason called for Mary, Lenoir's maid, who appeared as quickly and efficiently as Hank knew she would.

"She won't be back for a time since she's out with Mrs. Rodney and you know how they go on and on at art shows. It may be late," Mary said.

"I understand, Mary. I'll be in the library waiting for an hour or so. Otherwise, I'll come by in the morning."

"Of course, as you wish, Mr. Mason," she said and left him alone.

Settling into a wing-back chair in the long library that stretched the entire length of the house, Mason drank some brandy, leafed through *Time, Fortune, U.S. News & World Report,* and *Atlantic Monthly.* Lenoir did keep an excellent, up-to-date library, he thought, a trait from her father. Browsing the shelves, he savored the titles of the leather-bound English, French, and German classic literature, her father's treasured law books, and the voluminous records of financial transactions her father had executed. Wentworth Donahue had been the J.P. Morgan of his era, working his wizardry to merge companies and keep nations from financial chaos. Mason never felt completely at ease in this library which held the works of Donahue's genius. Donahue's aura was still here, surrounding him, making him a mere mortal. And Donahue was never such. He was too powerful, too enigmatic, too energetic to be fitted into life-size dimensions. Or was Hank just overestimating the man whose shadow was still cast over Lenoir's life—and his— in a way, especially tonight.

Mason's father-in-law had stood in this room often, recalling his ventures and expounding his successes, while Lenoir and Hank shook their heads in agreement and smiled at each other, their mutual thoughts taking them beyond the old man's reminiscences of Wall Street and upstairs to their bedroom. Remembering, Hank now felt ashamed that he had not listened, that he had not learned so much as he might have from Donahue, whose money might help save him from disaster.

Swaying as she walked, Lenoir Mason came through the open double doors of the library, followed humbly by Mary, who held a silver coffee service. Lenoir's long blonde hair spilled over her face and onto her bare shoulders, pink and blushed by the sun. Her eyes met Hank's in surprise. "I would have stayed had I known," she said, stiffening her body, trying to walk in a straight path to the chair opposite Hank's. "Are you here to go to bed with me or just to get a drink?" Her words slurred and rolled over a heavy tongue.

"I'm not here for either of those reasons, specifically. But I did get myself a drink," he held up his brandy. He was disgusted with her at first, and then his feelings bordered on pity.

"Well, I guess the bed bit doesn't apply, not with the waiting wombs you have at Airways. Let's see, there must be at least 2,000 of them and 4,000 tits. Yes, my arithmetic is accurate. I can still figure that out."

"Stop it, Lenoir. I came on business." He wanted to shake her, to take her in his arms and make love to her all in the same moment.

"Business, of course," she said, throwing her head back and

shaking the long silky mane of hair against her back. "Umm, that tickles."

"What? What was that?" he asked.

"I was talking to the ghost that tickled my back." She reached for the coffee Mary had poured for her. "Where were you when the lights went out?"

"The lights never went out between us. They only dimmed to this dullness. But I'm not here to talk about us."

Pausing, he searched for the right words. Then he got up and began pacing the room. "I've a business proposition. I need to borrow some money, a large amount, for a few weeks, at the most a month. You never like to turn down a good return on your money." What was he doing, crawling around in this vacuum? Why in God's name had he come? Now ashamed and bewildered, he felt he had somehow lost the war and won the battles all along the way.

"You were always too proud to borrow money when you first started that pissy little airline. Why have you come to me now, to the great Donahue fortune?"

"Because I don't know where else to borrow it on terms I can live with." He was getting mad, and inside fires were leaping from the ashes of his defeat.

Laughing, she rose and attempted, stumbling at first, to swirl about the room, her silk chiffon dress floating about her slender body like a wave of blue.

Trying to cool himself down, Mason purposely grew entranced by the shimmer of beauty in his midst, allowing himself to be held in her physical spell as a child is captivated by the mystique of a magician.

"How much do you want?" she asked after a long pause.

"I need a few million, and I can explain the details to your lawyers in the morning. But you have the power over your accounts. I wouldn't pull something devious on your bank account, Lenoir, and I wouldn't ask—but I am in a corner."

"You know, Hank, I believe you. The money, of course, you have it. What is money anyway? It has always been more to you than it ever was to me. You may deny that but it's true. I know. I know. Perhaps that's why we could never possibly be a team. I suppose you'll always be proving something about money, my sweet fool. Oh, yes, I have been drinking in the town. There is little else to do." Lenoir sauntered around the room, her words seeming to drip, slowly.

"There isn't anybody in your life?"

"Ha! You're incredible. You really are, Hank. You know this place is short on real men. And then there is Lenoir Mason who is in marital limbo. What are we, Hank, anyway? I'm not really sure." She glanced off toward the doors leading to the terrace.

"It's too tiresome, Lenoir. Let's not get into it. Let's at least be civil. You heard from Everett?"

"No, strange and wonderful that you should ask about our son. No, Everett is still in India, I believe. Since communications from over there are rather difficult, I do not hear often." Her voice was brittle and pretentious, and Hank wanted to escape from the room and from the memories and the pain of their failures in marriage and in parenthood.

Lenoir loped toward the terrace, shaking her head and lifting her arms to the ceiling. "Goddamn you. You walk in here unexpectedly and ask for millions with all the finesse of an elephant and refer casually to a human being that you created and have practically destroyed. You beast…the alcohol is wearing off. Get me a long, cool drink, now!"

"I should not have come here and I'm sorry, Lenoir."

"*Sorry!* How dare you?" Turning again, she began to laugh hysterically. As if by signal, Mary appeared and led Lenoir to the bronze cage of an elevator just outside the library.

Drinking and mumbling, Lenoir was propped against four large pillows on her bed. The doors to her balcony were open with the ocean in full view from the third-story room. Hank sat on her chaise lounge in a corner of the room, listening to her ramblings.

In these moments, when Lenoir drank beyond reason and talked without purpose or any trace of reason, he could do nothing but listen. And in the darkness he wept.

Alcoholic, nymphomaniac, genius, schizoid; she was all of these and more, doctors said. Psychiatrists were often perplexed by her facets and dimensions, all of which they said began back in Pennsylvania in the small town where they both grew up. Professional opinions relieved him of guilt, but he knew on occasions like this that no matter what doctors said, he had to carry some of the blame for her condition. If he had stayed by her in the early years of their marriage and seen his work in perspective, she might have never have resorted to other men and liquor and wasting herself with the empty, useless creatures of her moneyed class.

Lenoir was too reasonable, too balanced at times to be institutionalized. Like some of the mentally troubled people of her ilk and social stature, she remained outside, free, harmless, and labeled as her youth and beauty began to fade, as merely a wealthy eccentric who indulged herself a little too often in booze. The lasting tragedy of her life was that she did not want to help herself. Hank Mason admitted that to himself after years of pushing her into doctors' offices. Lenoir did not want to live in brighter lights, but instead, in a mirage, with only rare clear minutes. This was the most bearable existence to her, he had decided.

But now seeing her this way, he questioned his conclusion. Was it fair to let her go on like this? Should he get involved again, helping her recover a sane existence? There was always hope, he believed.

He wrestled with the argument. Where would he start again? Doctors, different ones maybe. Treatments—there were many new approaches to her problems. There were possibilities.

Visions of Lenoir as she was once many years ago roamed through his memory as he sat there in the dark. He put his head back on the chaise and thought of things as they might have been between them.

✈

"Did I sleep with you last night?" Lenoir asked Mason when she joined him in the breakfast room the next morning.

"No, I slept on the chaise lounge. Just dozed off there, I guess."

"I do remember the money you wanted, and I thought when I got up that a few million is a hell of a price to pay for a screw. And no matter what you did, how you performed, it would not have been worth that much."

Looking at her, he was amazed that she could live the way she did and still be a beautiful woman. Her fair skin was clear, her eyes were aqua blue, and her figure was flawless, without a ripple of loose flesh. Of course, she lived in spas and beauty salons, and she did swim and play tennis regularly. But it was still a wonder that she had not destroyed her looks with alcohol and the base men who made a folly of her bed. He supposed the demise of her beauty would come quickly, a kind of total destruction like the sudden collapse of a wall. He had seen that happen to women in his life, but he hoped she would go on looking as she did today. He could hardly keep his eyes off her.

"Yes, the answer is yes. I've called my attorneys. They'll let you know today how it will be transferred from my banks to yours and etcetera, etcetera. They don't want me to do it, though. It's against their good judgment."

"Don't make me beg, Lenoir." He felt a deep anger swell within him. No, there was no way they could be decent to each other. Her clawing cut him more than he allowed himself to admit.

"You have unmitigated nerve, Hank. You waltz in here. Ask for millions, and that's to save a company that helped ruin my life, and expect me to sit here and say, 'Yes, darling, of course.' What kind of moron do you think I am? Really, what kind?" She started to cry, and he knew she would go into a rage eventually if he stayed.

"Surely, you have other sources, other than my poor dead father and his skeleton of a daughter. You, Hank Mason, the greatest screw boy of the western world," she shouted. Her screams echoed behind him as he left the house.

Mason felt he had emerged from a nightmare, and he was sorry he had seen her and disturbed her this way. In the driveway, he stopped to tell Mary goodbye.

"I'm sorry it's always like this, Mr. Mason. Sometimes she's as normal as we are and other times…"

"I know. Let me hear if anything happens. If she does get worse this time, call me, Mary."

The mid-morning drive back to his office left Mason remorseful. His trip had only created more hostility. Yes, he had made the wrong move thinking Lenoir would help him without twisting his guts. After all, why should she? In the light of this sunny day, he wondered why in hell he had even bothered her. Obviously he was getting more desperate, more panicky than he realized, and he still had the problem. Maybe Whitefield was right. Resource the 747s and keep his staff. People were far more important than machinery.

Whitefield was waiting for him when Mason arrived at the office and so was a stack of messages which sat in the middle of the long table. "Whitefield, I have a plan," Mason said eagerly. "And I thought of it on the elevator."

"Hot air does rise they say."

"I'm not in the mood, Mr. Whitefield. This is a great plan. You'll like it. We're not selling and we're not cutting. We will lease some of our planes to that Middle Eastern country. They'll be short leases with options to buy. A maintenance contract goes along with each lease to the tune of ten supervisors per plane. That ought to ease our payroll. At least some." Mason was renewed by this alternative, and he was glad he could put Lenoir and her money in the back of his mind. At last, he was regaining the sense of purpose he had clung to most of his life. He had never sought the backing of Lenoir's money—he simply could not fall back on it now. There were answers in his own realm and, he had to maintain that belief and act on it.

"Then you did not get the money from the source you were so sure of?"

"Let's say I made a bad move there. But this plan will work, don't you think?"

"It might, but we need a pretty hot-shot negotiator with these Arabs. I'm not so sure of our broker in New York, Hank. You see he won't make the percentage on leases he would on sales, so his heart may not be in it. Realistically, it must be a quick deal. You might have to speak for yourself, but let's call him and find out now."

Mason's hotline rang then. It was one of Lenoir's attorneys.

"I've got a really serious problem, Hank," Porter Lamaretta shouted in his husky voice so that even Whitefield could hear him.

"Then Lenoir has told you about my visit and request?"

"Yes, but that isn't why I'm calling, Hank. It's a large, large amount. But that isn't the dilemma. It's Lenoir. I've had several reports from her doctors recently. Well, we have to come to some decisions about her competency, and I think it would be to your benefit now, especially now, since this money matter has come up..."

"I think I hear you loud and clear, Porter."

"Well, we understand each other then, don't we? I don't need to double-talk. And I'm glad. So many times these things are so delicate, Hank."

"I think we ought to discuss this another time, Porter. I've decided for the moment against the loan from Lenoir."

"Well, Hank, this decision, you know, is on a broader scale, and we ought to get some plans in motion," Lamaretta laughed. "A loan might be just academic. It might all be yours."

"I understand, Porter. I have to go." Mason slammed the phone down against the cradle. "Shit, another lawyer trying to milk an estate and make me an accessory. They're all prostitutes. The slime of society licensed to rape and steal."

"Is one of them trying to make you very rich in the meantime?" Whitefield said, looking Hank squarely in the face.

"We don't need to play games, Whitefield. Yes, I could be rich that way, I suppose. But you know I wouldn't have Lenoir's money even if it was a gift from her. I tried to borrow some, yes, because I'm running scared now. But I sure as hell better find another way. Let's try my idea on our Arab friends."

Whitefield shook his head negatively but dialed his secretary and asked her to put through a call to Kenneth Broderick, the broker in New York who often found short and long-term loans for the airline industry and sold older and excess planes when no one else in the United States could.

Chapter 3

Just after the New York call was placed and Whitefield and Mason learned that Broderick was out until later in the morning, Mason called his Washington attorneys.

"Where the hell do we stand now with the girls?" Mason paused for an answer. "I thought so. Look, I've decided to meet this Trina Bellam, the head of the union. I want to sit down with her and talk. What do you mean it's against policy? I'm changing the policy. Well, that's more like it. I want to meet her in Washington, Brazil, Hong Kong. You name it. And I don't want it to get around. I need complete privacy. Okay? Let me hear."

"You've just headed for a lioness's den. Do you really think talking to Trina Bellam will help you resolve a strike? She's a bitch, Hank," Whitefield said, rising from his seat at the table to get a glass of water from the wet bar near the corner cabinet.

"How do you know that? Have you met her?" Why must he fight the accepted codes everywhere he turned? Conclusions before investigations. Even Whitefield was bogged down in solutions by proven methods.

"No, but it is obvious she is antagonistic toward the airline and top management. Have you read what she's said to the press about our executives?"

"I'm not interested in what the press has reported or what she's said to anybody else. She's never spoken a word to me, and if she has the power everybody says she has, she must have some reason about her, some sense of business. Anyway, it can't hurt. I've never met a female union leader, have you?" Mason smiled. He ran his hand through his thick hair.

"Maybe it isn't such a bad idea after all, Hank. You might charm her right into a contract."

"Sure," Mason laughed. That was not an all bad idea. Not bad at all. "We'll see," he said, turning suddenly to answer his private line. It was Broderick, and Mason explained his plan to lease a group of his jets to the broker's contacts in the Middle East.

At the end of Mason's pitch, Broderick told him simply that he would have an answer in twenty-four hours and that his commissions would be jacked up to six percent of the total amount of the leases, and that sum would have to be paid at the front end of the deal. Mason agreed and that was the end of their two-minute dialogue. "I do like that son-of-a-bitch, Broderick. He sure doesn't waste your time," Mason said.

"No indication, then, that they will or they won't? That is, in Broderick's opinion?"

"No, we'll just have to wait for the rest of the day. I'm taking care of my desk work, and then I'm going to have a steak and some wine, and a woman. In that order. And how about you?"

"I am having some hamburger, a little ale, and my wife. I suppose in that order," Whitefield said, smiling.

"Your trouble, Whitefield, is that you do not dare. If it isn't on that computer run, you can't see it. You just don't use that old imagination." The predictability of his colleague amused Mason for a minute. And then it pleased him. If he could not count on the sensibility of his own actions, he sure as hell could on Whitefield's.

"I'll see you tomorrow," Whitefield said, gathering his sheets and putting them in white folders. "And don't forget to keep your doors locked." He pushed his glasses back securely against the bridge of his nose, looked at Mason who was studying the remaining drops of his liquor, and left the office.

Mason's thoughts drifted back to what his intruder had said of him the night before. He tried not to care about her low description of him. After all, what did she know except what grew from hangar and office gossip? People liked to invent wild tales about the men and women at the top of any company, he knew that. On the other hand, these tales, the ones about him, were not lacking in real substance.

Why did he continue to chase women, why couldn't he stop himself? Were his desires so insatiable or were bodies just a habit with him?

"Crap," he said. If there hadn't been a strike, he would never be questioning his own behavior. With renewed energy, he dived into a pile of letters he had to read and sign.

Francine La Per was the kind of woman Hank Mason had dreamed of in his puberty. She was bosomy and leggy and fleshy and wore black negligees with nothing underneath. When she knew Hank was coming to her apartment, which he paid for, she met him in one of those negligees. She did not speak to him when he arrived but enfolded him in her arms and kissed him with full ruby lips. Then they were lost for hours in the kind of rapture that divorces men from reality—and often from their wives.

That night as he drove to her place on the ocean in Fort Lauderdale, he thought of the women who had come after Lenoir, their faces and bodies fused together and faded into memory. He had not loved any of them and could not remember any one of them passionately, as he always remembered Lenoir. Their names escaped him, too, but it was easy for him to recall what they did. He knew his habit of picking up girls from his own employees was bad for his executive image, but what the hell. Weren't all of his stewardesses the best chunks of femininity on the market? And they were available to him. Any time, any place. Most of his girls considered it a real coup to sleep with Hank Mason, president of Airways. His executives passed the word back to him from the ranks, mostly, he imagined, because they knew it made his ego beam, and it did shoot their stock up in his eyes—momentarily.

For five years, Francine had flown for Airways. During that time, she once told Mason she had worked on Miami Beach as a call companion and in Miami as a model for girlie magazines when she wasn't flying. For the past year, she had given up such extracurricular activities to devote more time to Mason, who had noticed her on one of his flights to New York. When he wasn't occupying her time, he encouraged Francine to look for a permanent man, maybe even a husband, and had introduced her to some of his divorced colleagues. A few of them had shown interest in Francine, but until one of them laid claim on her, he was reserving this feast of a woman for himself.

"Francine," he said as they lay nude together on a pool mattress on the balcony facing the ocean, "what do you know about Trina Bellam?"

"I've seen her. Pretty in a quiet way. Smart, I guess. She heads our union. She's not your type, though." Francine rubbed his leg with her toes.

"If I want this union thing settled, I have to meet her and try to talk some sense into her, or at least hear from her what the union will really settle for."

"What about the people in Washington? Can't they do that?"

"They're doing a crappy job of it, Francine. Tell me what I should do about this strike?"

"You should maybe talk to her, I guess. I don't know. I wouldn't know how to handle it."

"You sure know how to handle everything else important, Frannie," he said, reaching for her full breasts. "I may talk to the whole union. What would you think of that?"

"Oh, God," she said and laughed heartily. "I don't think so. You, uh, have such a reputation. Well, you know how some of the girls feel about you. There's a kind of real thing against you now. I mean some of the girls who are, uh, you know, the libbers and maybe some of the girls you've left behind might not be nice to you. I don't know. I wouldn't risk it."

"So you think it would be a slaughter. Well, it's a slaughter any way you look at it. Come on. Let's go. I didn't come here to talk business."

Arm in arm they went inside through the large living room

doors and into her bedroom which also opened onto a balcony overlooking the water.

As they made love, she more passionately than he, Mason's thoughts drifted from the warm woman he held in his arms, from the breeze that glided over the sheer draperies and over their naked bodies, from the soothing wash of the sea against the shores—to Hawaii and Lenoir.

Years before, Lenoir and Hank Mason, honeymooning, lay in each other's arms in Honolulu. They listened for the swish of the palm fronds in the strong Pacific wind, and they smelled the sweetness of the plumeria placed around the room in huge bouquets. They touched each other, the newness of intimacy racing through them, urging them to consummate the vows they said back in Pennsylvania. Their lovemaking, their rhythms were perfect, as they told each other in liquid whispers their marriage was made by the fates.

For a few seconds, Francine became Lenoir as most of the women he made love to eventually did. But then the mystery and the fantasy were lost quickly when he reached his climax and began to look at the female he had just taken or given in to. There were lots of girls who did all the work and sometimes he found that gratifying. At times he got tired of being the lion.

Rolling over when Francine had satisfied him, he thought of the number of women there had been. God, he could not count them or remember much about any of them. In a way that was a shame since some of the girls had been charmers, beautiful women who had gone on to good marriages. He did remember that some of them had even sent him wedding invitations—for a final dig, no doubt. He laughed as the faceless parade of bodies flashed through his mind.

"Hey," Francine sat up against the satin-covered headboard of the king-size bed, "I didn't know I was so funny." She touched his hair.

"You're not funny, Francine, you're a lifesaver. A doer of good deeds and you'll be remembered in the chain of human history, my own at least." He laughed again. "I've got to get some sleep. I almost forgot—you all right with money? Need anything? Anything at all?"

"Well, I could use a favor," she said, leaning toward her nightstand for a cigarette. "My mother's sick. You know she lives up in Enterprise, Florida. She may not have long. I could use some money for her, to make things a little easier. They just released her from the hospital."

Watching Francine's face in the light coming in from the moon, Mason sat up. Her eyes were welling up with tears. "What can I do? Does she need more medical care?"

"She hasn't had the best doctors in the world up there. I've sent what I could, well, everything I have, to be exact. It's her heart and she's not that old. Fifty-nine."

"Make travel arrangements to get her over to the Ochsner Clinic and Hospital in New Orleans in the morning. Let me worry about everything else. Why the hell didn't you tell me that before when all this happened?"

"Because you've got your own worries with the strike and all. And besides, I'm supposed to be a good-time Charlie, no worries, just plastic. That's how men usually like their women, isn't it?"

Plastic—he was getting it from all directions. Maybe she was right. Maybe that's how he had thought of her and all the rest of them. For an inarticulate woman, Francine had hit him with an acutely right word. "You know, if I didn't know you better, I'd say you were being sarcastic. But I know you better than that and you're not. Maybe some men think that way. But, Francine, I care about you as a person. Let's not get into my head now, okay? Just get your mother over to New Orleans. It's Mrs. La Per?"

"Mattie La Per."

"Okay, Mattie La Per, it's off to New Orleans with you. Frannie, you better plan to go too. I won't be around much for the next week or so anyway. I've got a strike to settle and an airline to save."

"Thank you, Hank. If those girls really knew you, that strike would be settled tomorrow. There's never been anybody like you."

"God, I hope not!" Who was Hank Mason anyway? In the tangled labyrinth of his mind, there was no clear self-image. He was just a gnarled blur, but that would have to change.

Mason twisted and turned in the big bed until he was exhausted by his own unrest and finally fell asleep.

At dawn, Hank was behind his desk at Airways reading *Aviation Daily*. As he flipped the yellow sheets over quickly, he was able to digest the short flashes of Washington news affecting the industry and items about the airlines and the people who ran them. Sliding several issues to his side, he called Jacob Markowitz, senior partner in the law firm that acted as outside counsel to Airways in Washington. Markowitz was living in the executive apartment in the law firm's suite.

"What the hell's going on with these negotiations, with the union people and the mediator?" Mason shouted into the phone.

"It's a little early for this," Markowitz told him, yawning. "Allow me to awaken…gently." He yawned again. "Calm down, Hank, it's all arranged. You can meet with Trina Bellam tomorrow, although I advise against it. You may set the negotiations back even more. She's a hostile woman and you're too direct a target."

"You'll have to let me take that chance. I believe I have something useful to talk to her about. Anyway, the legal avenues aren't working either. Exactly where are you and our company lawyers with them?"

"You remember the points we were on two weeks ago—postnatal time off and dental benefits to be paid by the company, cost-of-living salary adjustments, the uniform approvals by them, and automatic increases in hotel and meal bills. Well, we're still on those points and sub-points."

"I haven't changed my mind on these issues." Breathing deeply,

Mason filled his lungs and felt his chest swell. The office smelled stale, and he was sick of being trapped here.

"Then, tell me, Hank, why do you want to sit down with Miss Bellam? What's to be gained if this will simply be an explosion of personalities? I still say you'll do more harm than good."

"Why? Because I want to meet the opposition and try to establish better terms between us. And I want them to be more realistic about their demands. I can just stand so many of these things they're asking for." Mason spun his chair around. He had to get out of his office. It was becoming a prison cell.

"You've never done this with any group before."

"I've never been shut down by a union for two months before. I've never been boxed into a corner by a woman and a predominantly female union."

"Join the age of women, Hank. You can't win with your attitude. I'm sitting here alone, no breakfast made, in a drab male apartment. Believe me, my attitude is changing fast. Okay, the meeting is set in Miami at the David William Hotel. Lunch, she says, at the Chez Vendôme there. That's Coral Gables, I guess. She's a reluctant witness, so to speak. That increases the risk of more problems. I urge you to go gently."

So Trina Bellam had set the time and place and she was against the meeting. Mason felt himself beginning to dislike what he knew about her. His stomach nerves twinged. Well, he had to give her a chance, he argued with his emotions. If he approached her with a negative force, with her feelings running about the same, they would get no place. He would have to hold back his resentment of her and her union, and he would have to remember Hank Mason was not in the arena for himself alone. The livelihoods of many people depended on his meeting with the woman who headed her union.

Chapter 4

Mason reared back in his chair, the gravity of his problems weighing heavily on lowered shoulders and reflected in eyes that were usually clear blue. Today they were bloodshot, and they felt dry and overused. He sat for a moment with both hands pressed against his angular face and finely chiseled nose. Touching his flesh caused him to think of himself the way he looked now. The thin body, the tense muscles of his legs and arms. He had not been good to his body in a long, long time. No golf, no tennis. Not even a walk. There was no time. His frame ached to run, to swim, to lose itself in sweat and pounding heart, but everything had to wait. He had to wait to start living again.

Hank hesitated before calling Whitefield in on the conference call his secretary said was coming in from New York. Tapping his fingers on his table, he piqued his mind. Suppose the Arabs said no deal. Then what? A deal with his wife's attorneys to declare her incompetent? Or would his idea of a straight loan work? He dialed Whitefield himself on his private line. "I'd rather you come in here and we'll talk from one end," he told his executive vice president.

With a quickened stride, Mason walked to his door and motioned Whitefield in. Whitefield seated himself by Mason at the table, and Mason pressed down a phone button. They waited to hear what Broderick had to say.

Broderick's tones were guttural and his voice filled the room. "Mason, the damn Arabs drive a bargain with hands on. They'll go your leases, ten jets—DC-10s and 747s—for six months, five million in advance. But wait for this. They want a seat on your board for this, and they want to be your lender for the next major loan at 14 percent."

"That's extortion!" Mason yelled. His face was flushed, and the veins in his neck swelled blue against his skin. "With the prime rate of interest down around seven, and a place on the board; Broderick, I've got a board to deal with on that. They'll buy the other things…"

"You want the deal or don't you? There's no room for negotiations. They've told me that already. They're not going to wait either. They've got another airline standing in the wings, ready to deal," Broderick said.

Mason and Whitefield could hear Broderick slurping liquid. They looked at each other with frowns.

"Look, baby, you're in a bind," Broderick went on. "You may not get those mothers in the air for the next three months, and then you won't be able to build up your traffic to use your whole fleet for the next eight months. And you gotta have a payroll unless you got a rich uncle stashed away I don't know about"

"Major loan," Mason said, "how much is a major loan to them?" He put a hand over his forehead. Numbers raced through his mind.

"At least 20 million fish. That's the smallest amount and that figure will appear in the agreement," Broderick said.

Whitefield folded his arms and eyed Mason. Then he nodded his head.

Despite the signal from Whitefield, Mason shouted back, "Tell them no deal. No way."

Whitefield's face turned pink and he stood up, shaking his head. "I don't know what you're thinking of, Hank, you've got a payroll and…"

"You heard me, Broderick," Mason said.

"I heard you but I think you're hasty. I'll tell them you'll roll it over in your sleep and get back to me when you can. I'll stall them for as long as I can."

"No way will I make this deal without negotiating with them. It's robbery," Mason said. A kind of madness raged in him, and he could almost hear his heart beating. He sweated and felt the water trickle from his armpits against his skin. There were always some damn bastards out there trying to rape you if you were down already.

"Think, my boy. Just think. Consider and weigh it all out. And cool down. Talk to him, Whitefield. You're a wise man. Hank is only brilliant."

"I will," Whitefield said in wilted tones.

"Who are these people anyway, Broderick?" Mason said, trying to glue himself together.

"You wouldn't know them if I told you. A group of oil magnates and you won't be able to say their names, but you will in time, especially with one of them on your board. They haven't decided which one yet," Broderick said. "I'm getting off the line now. Decide, boys, and let me know." The line went dead.

"We can survive and we won't sell the big birds," Mason said as if he were talking to himself. "We don't need to make a $20-million loan. We can make smaller loans at more frequent intervals. The way we have done."

"That is, if we settle the strike. If we don't, Mason, if there isn't a flicker of hope in the next few weeks, we will have to put all the managers on furlough," Whitefield said.

"I'll worry about that when we get there," Mason said. "Right now I have to call the Ochsner Clinic about a sick lady." He paused and then looked at Whitefield. "I know you don't like what I just did, but I couldn't be taken. I have not said no absolutely. And I would have to talk to the board about this membership proposal. They are all more sensitive about that than anything else—loans, plane sales."

The alternatives were seeping into his thoughts. No, he could not afford to turn anybody down if he wanted to survive. It is amazing what you will do, he thought, if you are held against the wall.

Standing at the door of Mason's office, Whitefield frowned. "I think we might be on a collision course with fuel going up, constant worldwide inflation, and a strike that just will not go away."

Mason looked away and out at the planes. "Maybe everything you say is true. Maybe."

"You're a stubborn man, Mason, and maybe that's why you're president, and I work for you instead of running this airline. But let's look at the entire picture, look down the road. You know what's happening to airlines. We won't live another ten years at this rate. There will be fewer airlines left, all results of mergers and prices and more government control. These are products of our times. Holding out now is a kind of death. I feel it. Being a man who lives by numbers and facts, I don't say that very often."

"I know what you mean, Whitefield, but something in my gut won't let me break down and be taken in and won't let me run completely scared."

Mason knew he had to stand strong now. He was at the dividing line. Give in at this moment and inch by inch, everything he had worked for would slip away beyond his control. He rubbed a hand over his flat belly. If he were old and ready to retire with a roll of flab around his middle, he might take a different stand. But he wasn't there and he hoped he never would be.

The maître d' of Chez Vendôme showed Mason to a corner table of the darkened restaurant. After he ordered a Scotch, Mason wondered if this was another of the union's tricks, if Trina Bellam ever really planned to show up to meet him. He felt silly, even ridiculous in the situation he had ordered upon himself. A chill ran over his arms, and he took a deep breath and caught the smell of the spicy cologne he was wearing as he inhaled.

On his second drink, Mason was sure that this was her way of telling him to mind his own business. Then as he lighted a cigarette, a slightly built, attractive girl arrived at his table.

He stood and waited for her to extend her hand. She did not, but instead nodded and moved into the booth. "I'll have a glass of white wine," she told the waiter.

Her hair was brown with what appeared to Mason natural streaks of blonde running through it. The wind had blown her short hair into soft waves which he was glad she had not brushed smooth. The effect gave her a casual, sexy look that he liked. Her dark brown eyes flashed as she spoke. Her face, with its fine features, reminded him of a fawn's, and he thought she was too young and too fragile to run a union.

"Well, we know who we are so we should get right down to cases," she said, cutting a glance at Hank.

"For openers, thank you for coming, Miss Bellam." His eyes met hers in a direct line, and he detected that she was nervous despite her assured mannerisms. That put him at ease.

"What have we to lose, Mr. Mason?"

"I just wanted to meet you and tell you my position on a broad scale. And I want you to know I am willing to work with you to settle this strike. Neither one of us can afford to go on like this for much longer." He studied the pretty, straight nose, the pink color in her cheeks. That wasn't makeup. She was a real beauty, but she seemed not to rely on her looks at all.

"I'm just glad you're not a member of the Mutual Aid Pact," she said.

"It may surprise you, but so am I. The pact is expensive. It drains the member airlines that are flying, and it prolongs strikes in spite of what the Civil Aeronautics Board says. So I agree with you."

"You may have to let your management people go, the grapevine has it."

"I may not, too. Are we in a contest of who can outlast whom?" He looked at her, waiting for an answer. "Why can't we settle this dispute?"

"It's your whole attitude, your whole personality, Mr. Mason, which is, I'm afraid, reflected in the whole company. You asked me."

He leaned forward and put his hands on the table. "Is the problem that personal?"

"Come on, can't you imagine the girls, that is the girls who have not been Mason girls, who despise your beliefs about women?"

"So, it's kind of a women libber thing, argument, that's built into the flight attendants' position?"

"That's part of it." She stared at him for what seemed a long time.

"My God, if you're talking about my so-called sleeping habits…"

"Nobody gives a damn how you sleep and with whom, but they do think your general behavior with stewardesses is indicative of a deep hatred of all women, and most of our members are female. The males among us are respectful of us and have empathy for us."

"Wait a minute, Miss Bellam." Mason sat back. He was bigger than this. And he had heard it all before, too recently. The repetitiveness made him angrier than the pronouncement, he decided. What am I, some sex deviate? Or a whipping boy? I suppose I'm just supposed to be settling some kind of middle-class morality issue which I am not and will not. "I think we're getting off the track. This is getting a little too personal."

"All right, we'll talk about the points of dispute, then. Start anywhere you want," she said.

"I yield to you. You start us off."

"Then we should begin in the background because that's where a lot of the roots of the issues are. Sometimes, points of negotiations, Mr. Mason, are merely outgrowths of differences, and they can be dealt with rather easily if the lighting and shading are changed."

"For one thing, our contract has been up for settlement a year. No mechanics, flight engineers, pilots, or clerical workers have waited that long for a contract agreement. We wonder why this wasn't handled when our contract came up for renewal. Was your counsel just too busy or didn't top management think we were important enough? Did they think we would just hang around and sign any old agreement?"

"You've made a good point. We were settling other contracts, Miss Bellam, but we should have moved faster on yours."

"And the uniforms we wear…we're not strippers, you know. These outfits, cut up to our underpants and down to our navels, make us all look like hookers. Is that the image you want for the airline? Or are you so interested in selling tickets that way you couldn't care less about the feelings of those who help you sell those seats? Don't you think we ought to have a say about what we put on our backs, or near them, anyway?"

"If I gave you approval authority, your group would never be able to make one decision like that. Women never agree about clothes. We'd have 2,000 different opinions."

"Only a few of the girls appointed to a committee would have the final power. The members could plan their own if they did not like the company selected dress. That would relieve the company of responsibility."

"Well, I suppose that would be a plus for the company. I never liked deciding on designers' presentations anyway. All right, that could be worked out."

"But this is hardly the most important issue. I think the most unnerving policy Airways has is its way of getting rid of women when they begin to a show a little age. Taking away our flight attendants' prized seniority when they have worked long and hard for it—now that's plain inhuman. No, finding them other jobs in the airline is not the answer. If they can fly and serve and keep up with the other girls, we should keep them where they want to be—on those airplanes."

Mason watched Trina's slender white hands begin to move as she talked, and again he eased back in his seat, listening to her. There was a deep anger in her and he let her pour it out. He thought when she sensed he was playing an omniscient role, she drew away from the lightning rod she had brought to the table.

"I promised myself I wouldn't get mad, and usually don't at the negotiating table," she said.

"We can talk about the other points another time if you like."

"I'm not an easy lay, if that's what you're thinking."

"You're too damned fired sure I am after all women, aren't you?"

"Aren't you?"

"I guess we should not have met after all."

"On the contrary, Mr. Mason. This proves my thinking—that we are worlds apart." She walked away from the table without looking back. Mason knew he could either go after her or sit there with the meeting blown. He froze and then he moved, slowly. He had never run after a woman in his life—except Lenoir. Who did this broad think she was? "I've got more at stake than she has," he said aloud, "so what choice do I have after all. Goddamn her."

At the front door of the hotel, he stopped her. "Look, come back a minute," he said. They stood to the side of the glass entrance doors. "Can't we sit down peacefully and discuss things? I don't like this atmosphere between us. I hope you don't. Would you mind meeting me in my office, say in an hour?" Had he actually calmed to this point? He asked himself as he waited for her to answer.

"I'll give it another chance," she sighed. "All right."

Driving to his office, Mason tried to size up Trina Bellam. Pretty. Smart. Quick. Defensive. Even an up-start. She was not a fawn after all—she was a tigress. Trying to prove what? Was she a man hater? He could not decide. Mason fantasized that they were in bed together. He had conquered her after an hour's struggle and she said to him in her sultry voice, "Strike, what strike? Union? What union?"

Less than an hour later, Trina Bellam and Mason sat side by side on his office sofa, he with an arm outstretched against the back of the furniture and she with her arms folded.

"What made you decide to be a union leader?" Already he felt he had won a point. She was here beside him, this strange mixture of desirable femininity who might be the key to solving the huge problem that clouded over his life.

"I guess caring about our union, the people in it, working conditions," she said, staring ahead at his table.

"Are conditions so bad here?" It made him damn mad that he

would condescend to ask her a question like that. His intestines writhed and twisted in testimony to his aggravation. Control, he told himself. Control. He had brought her here to talk, not to have a fight. That would solve nothing. He had to get his message across to her. Now or never.

Chapter 5

Trina Bellam stared at Mason. He saw no feeling in her eyes, and he was just not able to read her, to tell whether she regarded him as a human being or a serpent. "Tell me more, Miss Bellam, about why your union is holding out."

"We've been shortchanged by industry standards and general treatment, and we want that stopped. We are prepared to stay out until the management realizes its mistakes."

Mason started to seethe inside. Simplifying was easy for her, for the union. It was blatantly obvious the union had never gotten beyond its own desires, its own point of view. Trina was a stubborn outgrowth of the union's naiveté about the structure of business. They were using their force without reason, without understanding and worst of all, he thought, without the long view. She needed, her members needed, a basic lesson in how American industry worked. Telling himself to retrench, to try information instead of temper, he turned his body to face her.

"See those planes out there," he motioned to the windows, "they represent millions and millions and millions of dollars of investment. They're owned by shareholders. So-called little people. Some of them are flight attendants and mechanics and salesmen of this airline. I think management is prepared to rectify its mistakes, but do you know the price you're asking of us, the management and labor? We'll write an age, non-discriminatory clause into the contract if that's what you want, but you're cutting off your nose in the meantime with all these kinks in the talks…"

"I've heard all this before, Mr. Mason…that all jobs won't be here when the airline does crank up again."

"In this economy, with operating prices what they are, fuel tagged right out of sight, we'll have no other alternative than to cut back…everything. Do you know how long it will take to build traffic back? Does this mean anything to you?"

"Mr. Mason, who are you kidding? Of course it does. I love this airline," she stopped and looked at him, her face flushed. "I mean, it's given me a wonderful life"

"Then why are you girls trying to kill it?"

"We're not. We're made up of men, too, you know, and we're part of a bigger union run by men. The feminine gender is not the only voice."

"Miss Bellam, Trina, you're intelligent. Let's put our differences aside for a few minutes and look at a much bigger picture than what you want and what I want. Agreed?" His voice mellowed; perhaps, he thought, because he did not need to shout. He did at least see a crack in her veneer, didn't he? Or was he deluding himself, imagining a potential vulnerability in her? Well, she had said the airline had given her a good life—so there was some emotion, some feeling of allegiance to his company. He was beginning to get through to the human being trapped behind that I'm-all-business façade.

"I might be able to comprehend the big picture," she said.

"All right." He got up from the couch and stood with his back to the window, determined to avoid a comeback to her put-down. "When I started out, I had nothing. I was a pilot and dusted crops in Belle Glade and Pahokee, just north and west of here. I got a few planes together, borrowed some money from bankers, and set up a little airline that carried mail and a handful of passengers per plane around Florida. After a few years, the Civil Aeronautics Board said I could serve Miami and New York and Boston. And then I borrowed more money and bought more planes, all on credit. In the span of under 20 years, we have a sizable airline linking the East and Far West and Latin America. We have visions of going to Europe. Now, with the strike like this, I may be forced to sell some of our equipment which means a setback in the service we're able to offer and a detriment to the arguments we've begun in CAB cases planned to open up new routes to Europe. Worse than that, I'm going to have to furlough employees, and that will show up as bad news in our applications for new routes. And it will hurt those individuals involved—in the long run the whole economy." He paused, waiting for some reaction. When none came, he continued.

"The worst result of all could be that we get in a greater financial mess over the next year. That means the larger airlines, which are better capitalized—there are some, and you know which ones they are—will try to buy us out. They'll merge us with themselves and they'll be the survivors. Airways' identity would be gone and many of our people would be without jobs with the remaining airline."

The truth of what he'd said made him sad. To think it, to keep it all locked in the dark recesses of your mind is one thing. To verbalize it, to admit possible failure—the end—carried all the pain of steel blades going through your gut. There were tears of hurt in his eyes. He blinked, not giving in to his deepest feelings.

He paced back and forth, looking at the carpet and then at Trina, hoping for some understanding of his position. "The government of this country expects a nationalized airline industry one day, and you and I will live to see it if management and labor unions aren't reasonable in solving problems like this," he went on.

"So you're saying for the survival of the competitive airline system, give in, flight attendants, or you may have no jobs at all someday."

"What's wrong with a competitive system? It's the reason we are sitting here talking. You wouldn't be able to bargain and negotiate if the government ran the industry."

"Cool it, I believe in the system." Trina unfolded her arms and moved near Mason at the window. "Mr. Mason, Hank, I think I understand the economic structure of airlines in America and I know airlines are nationalized in other countries—and subsidized. I wouldn't want that in America. Not at all."

Mason found her nearness stimulating. In spite of the block that stood between them, he felt a sudden bond as they looked out at the hangar and the planes. Her eyes were calmer now. Her clear skin was pink in the light of his office. Was she retreating even a fraction? Well, at least he began to feel more relaxed with her. She did seem to have a perspective of the industry and that was in both their favors.

"Would you join me for dinner tonight?" he asked. His private line rang then, and he wanted to ignore it, but couldn't. As he moved away from Trina, he noticed she followed his limp.

"It's Mary, sir. I don't like to have to call you, but it's Mrs. Mason. Could you come up? She's gone and, well, I don't know where else to find her. She's been gone out for a day-and-a-half, and I don't want to call the police."

"Hold on, Mary," Mason rubbed a hand across his forehead. "I'll be there in an hour. Don't tell anybody about this. I'll find her." Mason hung up the phone and was lost for a few seconds in the new dilemma.

"Trina, I have to leave now. And I'm sorry I started this without getting anywhere. It's personal business. Look, we can talk again. Anywhere."

He saw the bewilderment in her eyes, and at the same time he sensed a concern. "Yes, okay, call me. This is my number." She handed him her card.

What had Lenoir done now and with whom? His insides shook, and he was frightened by the visions that flew at him.

When he arrived at Lenoir's house in Palm Beach, memories of years past and one year in particular came flooding back to him. He could feel his veins flowing with the kind of venomous jealousy and rage he had experienced when he first discovered his wife with another man. He returned to reason as he tried to tell himself that horrible chapter in his relationship with Lenoir was behind him. Lenoir was not really his wife now, and nothing about her should disillusion him. Should it?

"Mr. Mason, I am scared," Mary said, her hands shaking. "She went out last night about eight to a concert at the Flagler Museum. She never came back. It isn't like her to stay away this long."

"Where has she been going lately? Bars? Art galleries? Tell me every place you can think of and whom she's been seeing."

"Well, Ta-boo and O'Hara's, and there's this little ice cream parlor on Worth Avenue. It just opened this season. She's been going there a lot with her friends, well, mostly Mrs. Dansforth. Other than that, I don't know. The beach. She could have drowned," Mary sobbed into her apron.

Mason put an arm around the plump woman. "I'll find her. Don't worry. I won't stop until I do." After a call to Barbara Dansforth—a friend of Mason and Lenoir since they had come to Florida after their marriage—Mason learned that his wife had left the concert with a group of friends, any one of whom could probably tell him Lenoir's whereabouts. So said Barbara who, herself, had left the group about midnight, when Lenoir was still going strong and was reluctant to go home.

"Who's at a new ice cream shop I should know about?" Mason asked Barbara, but she was evasive at first and then too helpful, launching into a wordy explanation of the new ice cream spot, assuring him it was strictly for teenagers. Nobody *their* age would be caught in a place like that. Mason didn't believe her and headed for it first.

The ice cream parlor on Worth Avenue was in one of the vias that wound off the avenue and led to alcoves of art galleries and quaint gift and clothing shops. The ice cream parlor was empty except for a young man dressed in a red-and-white striped outfit. "Who works here besides you?" Mason asked. He tried to be casual, looking at the Tiffany-type lamp shades that hung from the ceiling and a completely mirrored wall opposite him.

"Who wants to know? Are you the police?" The young man put his arms on one of the wrought-iron chairs as Mason seated himself opposite the waiter at a marble-top table.

"Relax, I'm not the police or a private detective," Mason smiled.

"A friend of mine said he had a pal who worked here and asked me to say hello for him. Hell, I've forgotten the name he told me. He's heavier than you. I do remember that."

"You want coffee or something? The only other person here is Philip Johannesburg and he's off today. That must be the guy you're looking for. He's a big bruiser. Where are you from?" The young man went behind the counter, seemingly preoccupied, Mason observed, with arranging soda and sundae glasses on the shelves in front of the mirror.

"All around," Mason said. "Wherever I hang my hat, you know. Yeah, I'll take coffee." How on earth had Lenoir been attracted to a soda jerk, working here in this dainty setting? Mason asked himself.

"Here for the season to get rich?" the waiter asked, setting coffee before Mason.

"Ha! In this town? How can you get rich here? People come to Palm Beach to spend it not make it." Mason could feel the young man befriending him.

"You got a pad yet?"

"No." He paused, staring at the black coffee. "Look, I don't want to take your time. Where does Phil live? I could drop around and see him."

"We live together. But he's probably at the beach down at the end of the street. That's Sunrise. We're in one of those barns about ready to be torn down. It's the second one up from the ocean," the young man said, straightening a chair at Mason's table and looking at himself in the mirror.

"Thanks. Put it here," Mason held out his hand, relieved that the young man had given so freely of his knowledge. He left a crumpled bill on the table. "Thanks for the coffee."

As he left the via, Mason faced the disgusting picture of Lenoir and this Philip somewhere together.

The ocean block of Sunrise was old white houses, once

single-family retreats. After parking his car on the street in front of the house where Philip and his friend lived, Mason walked slowly to the open porch on which he found bicycles and weathered wicker rocking chairs. He wished he had not come—but he had to. His palms sweated, and he wiped them off with a handkerchief. He could not put this off now or get anybody else to discreetly fish her out of her hell hole. He felt her presence in there with some bronzed beach bum.

Just inside the doorway of the front porch, Mason found a row of mailboxes, one of them bore the name he was looking for. Apartment 1E. With a quickened gait, Mason walked down a dark hallway, the wood floor cracking under his steps.

He knocked softy at first and when he got no answer, he started to pound on the door.

"Who is it?" a voice yelled back.

"I'm looking for Lenoir Mason," Mason shouted.

There was stillness and then the door opened. Lenoir stood before him. Her blonde hair was matted, and it looked sticky, probably, he thought, from sweat and the ocean air. Her eyes were vague and unfocused at first and then she squinted at him.

"Oh, my God," she said, letting the man's robe she was wearing fall open to reveal her nude body. "Come on in and join the orgy."

"I think you ought to come home, Lenoir. Mary is worried." He was relieved she could stand up on her own at least.

"Hilarious. My maid is worried and you came here to tell me that. Oh, may the blue bird of happiness shit on your grave," she sneered at him.

Mason pushed the door open, moving her inside the darkened room which reeked of liquor and musk, old rugs and dirty, damp furniture. He did not try to locate the man whose voice had answered his intrusion but instead grabbed Lenoir by the arm and twisted her into a position in front of him. He wanted to hit her, to tear her into a thousand pieces, but he released her. "Come on, Lenoir. Now." He gritted his teeth, realizing he was torn between slinging her across the room or gathering her in his arms and racing away from this gutter with her.

"Just a damn minute," a broad-shouldered, muscular male said, coming to Lenoir's side. He was taller than Mason's six feet—and young. He put an arm on Mason's shoulder, and Mason felt the thrust of the man's strength.

"Who are you and what right have you got coming into my home and taking my girl away from me?" he asked.

"Legally, buster, this is my girl. She's my wife. Let go of her." Mason jerked his shoulder from the man's hold, and then he reached for Lenoir who pulled back and fell on the rumpled bed beside her. As she did, she kicked over a liquor bottle; its contents ran over and into Mason's shoe. The warm liquid oozed through his socks.

"Okay, okay. Give her a chance to go with you. You want to go, babes, or stay here?" Philip said to Lenoir. He stood there, a Goliath of a man, Mason thought. The damn bastard.

Mason looked at Lenoir on the bed, lying there, squirming like a snake, and he was sorry he had come to see her this way. "Goddamn you, you tramp, get up from there and walk," Mason screamed. He did not see the woman in front of him but instead there was the image of Lenoir of years before and the man whom he often thought was the father of Lenoir's only child. After he found them together in his house, his whole life had changed because he had allowed that scene to eat away at him. He hated Lenoir and himself for what they had done to each other.

Shaking his head fiercely to dispel those agonizing memories, Mason reached for Lenoir and dragged her from the bed, and she fell to the floor and bit at his leg. So fierce was her attack that his leg began to bleed, and when he looked at her mouth he thought he had struck her by accident. He knelt beside her and looked up abruptly. Philip was standing over him with a gun.

"Stop," Mason cried out. "Put it away. This is insanity."

"Maybe so, but I want you out of here. I don't care who you are."

Mason was close enough to Philip to smell the whiskey on his breath. This was no time to argue. Just as Mason was getting to his feet, Philip struck his head with his foot, thrusting Mason against the floor.

Philip lost his balance, and his gun fired. Lenoir screamed.

"I'm hurt," she moaned. She collapsed, her body falling crumpled onto the floor.

Chapter 6

When Hank Mason awoke, he was lying in emergency in Good Samaritan Hospital in West Palm Beach. The man leaning over him was saying something to a nurse. Both human images were fuzzy to Mason. "What is it? What's wrong?" The echo of his words rang through his head. He tried to move from side to side to get his bearings.

"Just a nasty graze on your arm and a cut on your face. You were knocked out pretty well. You'll be out of here in about 30 minutes though," the man said, continuing to wrap the arm tighter and tighter. The bandage tickled the hairs on Mason's arm, and he flinched from the sensation. Suddenly the whole ugly mess came back to him. "What about Mrs. Mason?" Hank looked at the man he assumed was a doctor.

"Mrs. Mason was wounded, and we'll tell you about her later. Just now, please, lie quietly for a few minutes." The room was still again, the nurse stayed, and he could see a table in the corner of the room filled with bottles and jars and medical instruments. Reaching to feel his head, he discovered a bandage on the right cheek Philip had struck.

"How bad is my wife?"

"Please, Mr. Mason," the nurse answered. "As the doctor said, be quiet now." She walked outside the room, and Mason stared at the white tile ceiling. The huge light overhead had just been turned off by the nurse. He heard muted conversations beyond him in the hall. Why the hell had all this happened? As if he didn't have enough problems. And Lenoir…was she critical or just superficially wounded as he had been by that moron Philip? Where was she anyway? Why wouldn't they tell him?

It seemed to Mason he waited for hours for the nurse and doctor to return, and when they did they looked at him matter-of-factly.

The doctor braced his hand against Mason's back to raise him up, and an aide appeared to help Mason into a wheelchair, to take him to another room for a brain scan, he was told.

"You seem all right, but we'll need to see you tomorrow. Mrs. Mason was wounded in the lower abdomen. She's in surgery, and we expect her condition to be stabilized after that. We will keep you informed," the doctor told him

"Thank God she's all right. When can I see her?" Mason said.

"Not until tomorrow. I'm sorry, Mr. Mason. And the full reports of the accident—the police, of course, have those. Again, I'll need to see you tomorrow to have a look at your arm and to give you a full report of our tests. We found a medical card in your wallet, and your doctor in Fort Lauderdale has been notified. You'll be released to him after tomorrow."

Mary was standing in the emergency waiting room, and she rushed to Mason and knelt by his wheelchair when she saw him. "Oh, Mr. Mason, how awful," she cried into her handkerchief.

Mason patted her head. "Let's go home now. We can't see Lenoir until tomorrow, Mary," he said.

When the Palm Beach police questioned Mason later that night, he told them the shooting at the rooming house was accidental and asked them to close the case as soon as possible, assuring them he would file no charges against Johannesburg. That was good, the officers told him, because Johannesburg had gone on record as saying the whole scene was accidental. Filthy scum, Mason thought, as he remembered the young bull who was obviously his wife's lover.

The story made the *Miami Herald's* front page the next morning—Mason read it at breakfast, which Mary prepared for him at Lenoir's house where he had spent the night. The *Herald* called Lenoir "the Donahue heiress," and the last paragraph of the short report mentioned that she was the estranged wife of airline magnate Hank Mason, who suffered a slight bullet wound in the accident. The truth of what had happened was there, Mason saw. He boiled inside as he read the story again and scanned another story in the *Palm Beach Daily News*. A phone call from Lenoir's attorney further angered him.

"I've got enough on my mind without you, too," Mason told Porter Lamaretta.

"But you see what is happening to her, don't you Hank? What will the outcome be the next time, when you are not there to rescue her? She could be kidnapped, sign away millions of dollars to any brute she goes to bed with. There are no assurances she won't do something very drastic. I wish you'd decide to become power of attorney. The documentation will involve only several days…and while she's confined like this…I urge you, Hank."

Mason put the phone down without responding. "Let's go, Mary," he said.

They drove to the hospital in comparative silence. Robert Whitefield met Mason outside Lenoir's private room. Her doctor told them that she could have one visitor at a time, that she was responding well, and that she probably could go home in two weeks or so.

"I won't ask you anything about this, Hank. I'm just glad you're alive," Whitefield said. He placed a hand on Mason's shoulder.

Her usual good color was drained from Lenoir's face, both cheeks showed blue-black bruises, her lips quivered when she tried to speak, and she could not turn to look at Hank but reached for him. "I'm grateful for what you tried to do, but I'm not worth it, you know," she said. Her eyes were half closed as she spoke, and she winced in pain, her hands clenching into fists.

"It's all right, Lenoir. Just forget everything and get well," he said soothingly.

Drifting in and out of sleep—induced, he imagined, from sedatives—Lenoir seemed a helpless child that he needed to protect. He had tried, hadn't he, to save her and to what end? Whatever he did for Lenoir was wrong. He had to leave because he could not bear to see her this way, in a condition that he had caused.

Outside, Mason directed Mary to go in after him, and he told Whitefield they could meet back at Airways.

In his office at noon, Mason hassled with the alternatives in his life. The easy way out, financially, was to take the reins of Lenoir's fortune. He could lend his airline, or himself, any amount of money he saw fit—if he did that. The lawyers, of course, would be able to take off a few million for their shuffling of certain papers, and their son, Everett, would continue to be protected by three separate trusts his grandfather had set up when he was born. No one could really get hurt. Lenoir would still have more money than she could use in five lifetimes. The responsibility of overseeing the estate would simply be Mason's and not his wife's any longer, he comforted himself.

If he did not declare her mentally incompetent, he might be the loser. Either the Arabs got their deal or he lost the support of his managers and his prize jets. Struggling with his thoughts, Mason again struck on the only real way out—he had to settle the damn strike. There was no way of getting around that.

Mason instructed his secretary to set up another appointment with Trina Bellam for the next night. This time it would be dinner and he picked the place, his suite at The Breakers in Palm Beach.

Trina Bellam was punctual. She arrived with her red leather attaché case and, what seemed to him, sincere sympathy for Mason's injury and his wife's accident.

"I'm sure you're broken up over that," he said, holding up his arm. "I can still sign things like contracts. And my brain isn't rattled, they told me today."

She smiled, her eyes crinkling at the corners.

"I didn't know you could do that," he said.

"What?"

"Smile, laugh."

"Don't let the crack in the iceberg give you any ideas," she said, opening her briefcase and setting a few papers on the coffee table of his living room. "Mr. Mason, I've thought about what you said and you present a viable case. Not just for settling the strike, but for holding the line against forces that could one day see the end of competitive air transportation in this nation. So, I think you should talk to our union."

"Oh, no you don't. I've been warned about that." Mason threw up his hands.

"I thought it was out of the question, too, until I really considered what you said. These things should be explained to all of our members and to all union members, to all employees. They may know some of what you said, but for you to stand before us and talk with us about these issues, that might break down some barriers pretty fast."

"Suppose I got shouted down by your union officials, your friends. This may be fine with you, but what about their attitudes toward me?"

"Well, I can't give you any assurances there will not be any ugly confrontations, but after your talk I'm betting we can negotiate more intelligently."

"The woman-scorned reaction is going to be put away then?"

"I can't say we're going to be sweethearts on the issues," she tapped her fingers on the papers, "but the atmosphere might be friendlier."

"All right, we have a deal," Mason said and they shook hands. "How about that dinner?"

"No," she answered.

The scent of her perfume lingered between them, and he felt an urge to insist on dinner and a drive along the ocean. No, he told himself. Don't push your luck. He sat back on the sofa.

"Another time, maybe," she said.

"What do we have here?" he said, leaning toward the table.

"Some information on the Kelso plan for purchase of stock by employees. I thought you might consider such a program for us. We can't buy stock through any formal company plan now."

"Let me see what you have. I know about these programs. I'm not sold on the effects, but it's worth a study maybe. Let me keep these. I take it you think this kind of thing would work at Airways?"

"Why not? Don't you want employees working harder and investing for themselves? This is one way it can be done. Spread the wealth and the risk around."

Mason studied Trina's face for a moment. "What makes you so concerned about employees and programs like this?"

"I care about things going on around me. And people most of all. My motives aren't complicated."

"And you're one of those women libbers, I know."

"I don't have to identify with a group of women libbers to know what's right and to figure out what I want, Mr. Mason. I knew long before women's lib was ever dreamed of. I knew as a child."

"Oh, did you? Well, you're a real visionary, aren't you?"

"I really do have to go, and you must need some rest after your accident. I am sorry about what happened. It must have been awful."

He did not want her to go, to leave him alone, and yet she was impersonal, removed from his sphere of problems. Unlike most of the women he had known, she kept a defined distance. Yes, of course, he admitted to himself—he was intrigued by that.

"It was," Mason looked away, remembering. He was suddenly tired and disgusted and unguarded. "You know, Miss Bellam, Trina, life can be one goddamn shaft. Here you are all locked in one body, and you can't seem to ever get off at the right place or tie it all together in one neat package. Loose ends. There are always loose, nasty ends. Am I making any sense to a sweet, young, dedicated, right-on-track person like you?" he asked, looking again at her.

"I think you are, Mr. Mason. I think you are." She packed up her briefcase with the other papers from the table.

"Do you have a boyfriend or husband or someone?"

"I have someone, sometimes."

"Does that mean you have lots of friends and no one special?"

"Could mean I just have a lover when I want him or…"

"He must be married then. And you see him when he's not home with his wife and kids. I thought you were smarter than that. I thought you were a 'new woman' who moved with the pace of the male animal with no emotional strings and all that."

"You think in images, and you've been listening to the wrong talk shows," she said.

"How about a drink before you go home or to Mr. What's-His-Name?"

"No, thanks."

"Trina, if I were as bad as some of your people think, I'd be in the hospital from exhaustion half the time."

"I think I know all about your habits, Mr. Mason. You've made them common galley talk."

He could not detect why she had become so brusque so quickly. "It's ugly. The story of Hank Mason. I know. Even Hank Mason thinks so." Pausing, he realized he did care what her reaction was to that statement. And for a time he was sorry, deeply sorry that he was this person that had become Hank Mason, president of Airways. In the last analysis, he had to live with himself. Not Trina Bellam or any other woman.

"I didn't mean to hit quite that low," Trina said, rising to leave. "I don't want for things between us to get brittle. Really, I usually don't attack people in that way. Let's say I made a mistake."

"Forget it. When do I speak to your union?"

"You'll hear from me soon. Good night for now."

He watched her leave and was left with his own silence. Walking around the room, Mason's thoughts centered on Trina Bellam. He had never known a woman like her. Intelligent, hard driving, reserved about her private life. She was old-fashioned and ultra-modern at the same time. He wanted to break past that cold surface and get to know her, but taking her to bed, or even trying to, was not the way. That may have worked with most of the females in his life, but he knew this was not the approach to use with her.

And on the other hand, why should he bother trying to get through to her at all? She was a means to end the strike, and when the labor dispute was over, they would probably never meet again. After all, she was not his kind of woman, and she had made it clear she was not interested in him as a human being, as a man. Their talks were all business.

Lenoir Mason's bullet wound did not heal at the speed her doctors had predicted, and when Hank Mason was told that she would be kept in the hospital another week beyond the anticipated two, he grew worried.

"What the hell do they know, Whitefield?" Mason said as they sat in Mason's office. "One minute the doctors tell you she's fine, and the next time you hear there are complications. Crap," he said, fumbling with some computer sheets on his table. Knowing himself as he did, he viewed his reactions growing more from fear than anger.

"What are the complications?"

"Doctors' terms. How do I know what they mean? For one thing, she is deeply depressed. Well, why not, I guess... Look, White-field, I've made my decision on the Broderick deal with the Arabs. We're not leasing any planes. Let the Arabs have the 747s, buy them outright. That'll be the cash in the till we need to keep our managers for a while. Then, if the strike doesn't end, we'll sell more planes. I just won't tie up loans, directors' seats, and be screwed generally by those sons of bitches. Tell Broderick I said that. I don't want to talk to him." Turning away from Whitefield, Mason said in a low voice, "I just want to be alone now."

Whitefield nodded, crossed the room, and closed the door slowly behind him.

Sitting quietly in his office, Mason rubbed his hands together. Walls seemed to be caving in on him at this moment. Everything and nothing. Nothing and everything. But now everything was far away. There was tightness in his chest as if his body were being closed off from functioning.

He loved the 747s. He would need them on new routes if he won them, he told himself. But there would be newer 747s and what the hell, his weren't moving off the ground anyway, hadn't in two months plus. Food in the mouths of the men and women who were manning the fort now was more important than the mothballed big birds. Still, he thought, it is losing to have to get rid of your equipment…

About an hour later, his secretary buzzed Mason. An Ashley Channing was outside waiting to see him, he learned. She was in advertising and in town from New York for a few days.

"I don't know her, and I don't want to see her… Oh, all right, send her in," Mason conceded.

Ashley Channing, a shapely woman—in her early thirties, Mason imagined—breezed into his office as though she owned the place. Offering him a strong hand with fingernails lacquered bright red, she took a seat on his sofa without being asked to.

"What can I do for you?" Mason asked. She had some nerve, Mason thought, as he watched her cross a pair of beautiful, tanned legs and smile at him with a remarkably pretty face. She looked like some toothpaste ad model, he decided. Too good-looking for everyday life. "Who the hell are you anyway?"

"Well, I know who the hell you are, so we don't need intros there. I am Ashley Channing, president of Channing-Brown Advertising, New York."

"Oh, yes, I've read about you in *Advertisement Age*. Former model turned girl wonder of Madison Avenue."

"Thanks, Mr. Mason. You're the one with the strike, a long strike, and no hits, no runs, and all errors."

"All right. What can I do for you? I don't have anything to do with advertising. And I sure don't need advertising. I don't even have an airline to run at the moment." He motioned his hand to the rows of planes outside.

"But you will soon, and you will need a brand new, marvelous campaign. My campaign." Moving to the edge of her seat, Ashley Channing propped her face on one of her graceful hands.

"I thought you people went through our marketing department. I never had any advertising person come directly to me."

"I'm different," she said. "I know you have a firm, a big firm in New York handling your account. I think they're doing a lousy job for Airways. Their sexist campaign, I would imagine, helped those girls decide on staying out as long as they have. You need adverting that your flight attendants will like, the kind that won't keep them in their sex-object roles forever."

"That campaign has won all kinds of awards and has had people talking about Airways for over a year."

"My own research tells me your flight attendants hate it, and it's helped ground your airline for over two months—and who cares how many people are talking if you're not making a dime?"

"You know, Miss Channing, I need all this discussion like I need a hole in my head. I've already got one, by the way."

"Funny, so have I. Can I buy you a drink then, since we have so much in common?"

"This is a damn crazy day. Did I send for you or something? Have I ever met you before?"

Her laughter seemed to light up the room, and her eyes danced with an invitation to Hank Mason to leave the office with her and go exploring.

"All right, I need a laugh right about now," he said.

Sitting across from Ashley Channing in the Captain's Lounge at the top of the airport terminal, Hank Mason wondered if he was losing his sanity. Here he was with an advertising executive who was hell bent on selling him a multi-million-dollar bill of goods, and he had a wife in the hospital, a strike in limbo, and a mountain of financial problems. "I'm losing my mind," he said half aloud.

"I lost mine years ago. It's the only way to survive in this world, Hank Mason. I thought you were sane enough to know that. Nothing, absolutely nothing, is logical or fair or reasonable today. Maybe nothing ever has been."

There was an iridescent quality about Ashley, Mason observed. Her green eyes sparkled. She was like a Christmas tree ornament, reflecting an array of color and gaiety, and yet there had to be substance underneath. He had heard more about her than he admitted when they first met. She was one of the highest-paid ad people in the country, which gave her about half a million in salary a year, more than triple his annual earnings. The TV ads her firm did were silly, he thought, but they had won her award after award. The question was what could she produce for Airways? Especially now.

"Whenever you want to talk about business, let me know," Ashley said. "I have plenty of free time just to have a ball, too."

"You on vacation here or what? My secretary said you…"

"Well, I had to get in, didn't I? I'm sort of on holiday. I came down with a photographer to shoot some stills for magazine ads for the hamburger chain account we won."

"You've never had an airline account before?"

"No, but I have lots of brilliant ideas."

"Such as?"

"When do you want a presentation?"

"I told you I don't handle things like that. If I did, I wouldn't be wasting my money on the people I've hired to do advertising. My marketing people tell me what the ads will look like. Sure I look at general themes, but hiring an agency, that's their business."

"You should make it your business," she said, tossing her auburn hair so it hit her shoulders. She ordered another Scotch and water.

"You should talk to my vice president of marketing, and then he'll talk to me." Mason leaned forward in his chair. "Not that I haven't enjoyed meeting you."

"The day isn't over, is it? With your airline on strike, what can you do? Labor negotiations aren't your bag either, are they?"

"No, they're not, but I have other things to do."

"All right," her voice was whimsical. "I've given you some free advice. Why don't you invite me to dinner, and I'll give you some more?"

Only because he had no other plans, he told himself, did he agree to grant Ashley her blunt request.

They ate at the Sky Club at the airport. His thoughts drifted off to Lenoir and then to Trina Bellam and to the Arabs and the sale of his 747s. Rambling on, Ashley talked about her childhood in Texas, her puberty in Manhattan, and her early success as a photographer's model. He imagined that she had told the same story the same way to many other company presidents, and they had all laughed when he did and sat in mesmerized wonder at this jewel of a female who was showering them with her attentions. He couldn't say he minded her little performance. It swept him away from his own problems.

In spite of her mechanical ritual, Mason found himself intrigued with her beauty and animation and zest. After three Scotches, he suggested they drive along the ocean, and she made the counter offer that they go over to the beach-front condominium in Fort Lauderdale which she had borrowed from a friend for the week. Mason could not propose anything better, and so they tooled over in a white Mark IV Continental, also her friend's she said, to the high-rise on the ocean.

The evening was a web of Debussy on the car radio and on the stereo in the apartment, a glittering penthouse filled with modern furniture and potted trees complete with oranges and lemons, and the excitement of Ashley amidst it all.

In the moon-silvered night, Mason lost himself to Ashley's

feathery touch, her soothing stroke. He glanced at her slender body when he awakened the next morning. Bathed in bright yellow sunlight, the bedroom was stocked with hanging baskets of ferns and tall palm trees, pastel paintings of French garden scenes, and white wicker furniture. Smiling at Ashley, who was still asleep, Mason got up and walked to the huge windows which offered him a full range of the Atlantic Ocean as it met the new horizon.

Ashley joined him at the windows, announcing that breakfast would be on the terrace.

"I feel like I'm in a magazine," Mason said, standing in the center of the living room decorated in chrome and glass and white plush rugs.

"The owner does publish a magazine, among his other ventures."

"Are you one of them?"

She laughed. "Of course. Why not? But I could be persuaded to broaden my activities. What about seeing your VP of marketing sometime today?"

"He's free territory."

"I can tell him you recommended me then?"

"Recommend you for what?" He smiled at her as she stood with her hands on her hips.

"I rather like you," she said, turning away to get his coffee. "Here," she handed him a cup. "And I think you like me, too."

In the midst of one of the worst periods of his life, Mason felt whole at this moment, as though the sea had parted and served up an island for him complete with this remarkable creature. Being with Ashley Channing was a new kind of experience. She seemed to take challenges as she found them, and that applied to him. "What do you do when you're not pursuing new accounts?"

"You mean do I enjoy all of my prospective clients? Of course not. I know all about you, Hank Mason. How you started the little airline you nicknamed the honey-wagon because you dusted crops in the beginning. Oh, yes, I know what a honey-wagon is. My dad was in the Far East right after the Second World War and he told me. They're wagons that collect waste, and they carry it to the fields for fertilizer. And let's see, you're married to an extremely wealthy woman who has tried to commit suicide several times, they say. I know the Palm Beach crowd and word does get around."

"Then you must know, too, that my wife is very ill now. She was injured in an accident in Palm Beach."

"No, I didn't know, but then I haven't really kept up with the papers down here. Intentionally, I need a break from the tragic news we're fed every day. I am sorry."

"I was trying to forget about my wife and the accident. I didn't mean to dredge up bad news."

"If you don't want to talk about it, we won't... I was just going to say that I think we ought to have something to eat now."

After a breakfast of eggs Benedict, Ashley's specialty she said, Mason called his man in charge of marketing and set up a luncheon appointment later that day for Ashley. "When will I see you again?" he asked when he finished the call.

"Any time at all you want to. In New York next time, maybe."

"All right, New York it is. In fact I have business there. We'll have dinner Saturday night. I'll be at The Pierre."

Chapter 7

Before Mason headed to his office that morning, he drove to Good Samaritan Hospital to check on Lenoir's condition.

She was stable, the nurses told him, but her doctors had given her sedatives which would keep her asleep for several more hours. There was nothing he could do, he decided. When he left the hospital, he felt dejected, as if he were walled off from the woman who had once been his wife.

"Damn," he said aloud as he drove away, "She'll be all right. She's got to be. She just hasn't lived her whole life. She couldn't have. Not this way."

Trina Bellam had called Mason three times, his secretary reported when he got to his office, and Broderick and Whitefield had made a deal with the Arabs to collect a $5 million down payment when the 747s were delivered to New Orleans in another week.

Whitefield was in the process of polling the board members to get their approval of the sale of the jets, Mason found out from his executive vice president.

When Mason reached Trina at her union headquarters in Miami, there was an excitement in her voice. "I've put feelers out, and we've scheduled your appearance for tomorrow night. We had planned a meeting anyway, and the consensus here is that maybe this is the right approach. We want to give it a try. You haven't changed your mind?"

"Hell no, I'm happy about this, Trina. If the strike ends, I'll owe it and the members of the union will owe it to your courage."

"I'm not so sure it's courage," Trina said. Her voice sank and Mason sensed she was waiting for him to say something to reassure her.

"After this is over, I want to do you a favor. I don't yet know what it could be, but I'll find something to do for you."

"No, I don't want any favors, Hank, just to see the strike ended sensibly. That would be reward in itself. Some things have been happening to some of us recently…" She stopped and Mason could feel that someone had come into the room and was listening to her. "I have to go." She was suddenly abrupt, and Mason began to have doubts about the meeting.

"Be at the union hall at seven. A committee will meet you. I may be there…but I can't promise anything…" Then she hung up the phone without saying good-bye to him.

Later in the day Whitefield urged Mason to abandon his plan to meet the flight attendants. "Let me take the chance," Mason argued. "Nobody else here has done anything, and I felt like firing every one of these damn attorneys—they've done nothing but sit on their fat asses throughout this whole mess."

Whitefield threw up his arms, but Mason knew he could not resist the comment. "Go ahead," Mason said, "let me have it."

"Well, since you asked. What can happen is not completely up to the members of the union. You remember the flight attendants are affiliated with a larger union and it can be vindictive if its mandates aren't followed. I'd never show up there tomorrow night. But it's your project, Hank, and no one can stop you."

Mason poured himself a double Scotch and dropped into his leather chair, propping his feet up on the table. "If I ran scared every time somebody warned me of the consequences, I'd still be a virgin, and I'd still be in Pennsylvania probably shoveling coal or working a truck farm. Not that there's anything wrong with either. I just had too much of both of them as a kid. Shit, Whitefield, life is one great risk."

Whitefield shook his head and folded his arms. "I'd better get back to talking with the board."

Just before six that night, Mason's general office phone rang, and what seemed to Mason a male voice half-whispered to him, "Don't show up at that meeting tomorrow night or you'll regret it." There was a click on the other end before Mason could respond.

He held the phone for a minute before setting it down. "What kind of bull crap…" his voice trailed off. Probably some coward who got the word through the union about Mason's plea and didn't want the strike to end, Mason told himself as he left his office and drove to Francine's. It wasn't the first time he'd gotten an anonymous call like this. As president of a company that employed 12,000 people, he knew he was vulnerable to all kinds of strange verbal attacks. And other kinds, too, these days.

His thoughts turned to Francine—she had called him from New Orleans and said her mother was hospitalized with gall bladder problems. Her heart, they found, was not her major illness. Francine came back to Florida to get in a few trips in case the strike ended, she said, and to see him while her mother stayed at the hospital for treatment.

Francine embraced Hank at her door. "Thanks for everything you did for my mom. They're taking real good care of her," she whispered into his ear and then kissed him all over his face.

That night she bit at his ear and that impelled him toward more intense force. When they had made love several times, he asked her to take a walk with him along the shore because he did not want to sleep. For two hours they played along the water's edge, flirting with the waves which broke four or five feet from them and sent white foam to lace the sand. Pulling her down under a palm tree, caressing her face and holding it in a kiss, he wished that she were someone else—Ashley or Trina. He let Francine go gently. She lay silent under the tree, its fronds casting shadows of fringes on her bare legs.

"I've heard maybe things won't be so pleasant tomorrow night at the union meeting," Francine said.

"Hell, things are never pleasant anywhere for me lately. Where did you hear that? I thought you weren't interested in the union or anything concerned with it."

"Well, a friend of mine was over here today, and she said she heard there's a kind of a split growing in our union. Some of the members want to stick it out and hold out for everything they want. The other group, I guess the one backing the leaders, wants to settle and start up the airline as soon as possible."

"What else did you hear from your friend?"

"Nothing much. I can't get too excited over all that. I can't see arguing over all these points. But I guess it's important. All I want to do is fly my trips and get paid."

Mason wondered why Trina said her contacts told her the membership would listen to him. Was she polling just her followers? Was she deceiving herself as well as Mason? He could never forgive himself if he caused her to lose her leadership in the union because of him, but he had to get the damned strike settled and he had to take his chances, too, with the union.

"Francine," Mason said as he lay awake just before dawn, "tell me more about your mother."

"They're giving her special treatments, and if they have to remove the gall bladder, well, she understands. But most of all, I'm just glad she's there. They know what to do. And that doctor back home! Well, I guess he's okay. You know she could have died. You saved her life."

"Not me. The good doctors. And I want to know how she is from time to time. All right?"

"Sure, but why are you doing all this for me? You're going to an awful lot of trouble for somebody you just sleep with. I can't ever repay you. Some favors are just so big there's no way you can match them."

"Forget it. Get some sleep," he said.

"You don't have cold feet, do you?" Trina asked Hank when she called him at his office mid-morning.

"Nobody's every accused me of that before. Do you have any reservations?"

"No," she said. "None at all."

"Have you had any more reactions today…are you going to be there? It would make things smoother."

"I've had a few comments, but nothing vile. Most of us here are eager to get back to work, to tell you the truth. I don't know if I'll be at the meeting. I should play all this from behind the scenes. For everybody's sake…but I may decide to put in an appearance."

Well, he could not push her. He had the meeting and that was what mattered most. Of course, it would not hurt to display to members that he and Trina did speak, at least.

After his talk with Trina, Mason instructed his secretary to hold all incoming calls. He took a yellow legal pad from his credenza and began to make notes for his talk to the union.

After making several attempts at writing his opening remarks, he wadded up empty sheets of paper and hurled them at the waste can and tried to begin afresh. It was no use. How had he phrased it for Trina? That's how he had to say it all for the union. Nothing written down. That would be too formal. Allow them to ask questions. Get a conversation going. That was the way, he assured himself.

Leaving his office, Mason tried to forget about the night that lay ahead of him and took the main elevator down several floors to traffic and sales. He nodded to the men who sat behind desks in the bull-pen offices, all open space with no partitions and no walls. The department was broken into sections, instead, by tropical plants. His vice president of human resources told him that well-defined compartments were passé and people showed superior performances in an atmosphere like this. The advice seemed to be right—the Airways sales team outsold all competition on the New York-to-Florida run and on flights between the West Coast and Florida, as well as those from Florida to Columbia, Argentina, Peru, and Brazil. But that was before the strike. Mason wondered, as he looked out over the empty desks, where secretaries and clerical people usually worked, and when this department would run at peak again. For a minute his mind's eye saw shadows of men and women who were usually here—mapping out strategy for the Airways sales offices scattered around the country and in South America, and even in Europe where they were trying to build Airways' name for routes they hoped to serve from the Continent and Great Britain. Mason remembered the frenzy of this place, for here sales brochures were written and designed, special tours were booked, sports and military charters were sold, sales blitzes were born.

But now, all of that life force was gone. Yes, the supervisory staff was working, but it was doing only the routine reports and answering phone calls from travel agencies or the public curious about the status of the strike.

Mason went to floor after floor, offering a hello here and there, digesting the quiet now in the reservations center, the computer rooms, public relations, advertising, accounting. He wound up his walk in base overhaul, where the work benches were empty, the hand tools put away in lockers of the mechanics who, like all other union employees, were honoring the picket lines of the flight attendants. There was hollowness in the base shops and in the hangar which usually roared with the clanks, the bangs, the gushes, the booms of keeping engines and aircraft in shape.

Supervisors, many of whom were long before promoted beyond their beginnings as line mechanics or base overhaul bench men, had taken off their coats and ties and were wearing overalls to wash fuselages and grease parts and change tires and tear down landing gears. These were among the hundreds of routine jobs that had to be logged to maintain the fleet, even grounded.

Mason waved to a few men on the monorail that ran hundreds of feet above him and around the jets. Platforms were extended from the monorail, and these allowed the men to work on whatever part of the planes they needed to. When the hangar was first built, Mason used to stand beneath the monorail watching the small golf-cart type cars speed the mechanics to the giant wings or huge bellies of the aircraft. Mason liked remembering his golden days. Would times like those ever come again?

The people, the machines, the typewriters, the computers, the phones—he had put them all together. He had created thousands of jobs, dreamed of and won new routes, designed special fares and package vacations. His colleagues had worked with him to carve out a thriving business that usually worked, despite union problems and government interference and controls. These days the government involvement was bad, but it did mean he had to build his own bureaucracy to keep up with Washington paper-work demands. In all, the government regulated his industry too strictly, Mason thought. At times, he felt he was running a race with weights tied to his feet. Where was the government now, when he really needed help?

All of this success was in jeopardy, he thought as he kicked the tire of a DC-10. Maybe not tomorrow and not next year, but this could be a graveyard in time, or the open field it was once—or Airways could be swallowed up by a bigger airline and no one would ever remember the name of his company, or his name. You're insane to think that you or an extension of you can live forever, he told himself.

The union hall was two miles west of Miami International Airport and as he drove there from his airline's base, he wondered if Trina would show up. He was beginning to feel the need for her but if she wasn't there he had to face the members with all the gall he had in him.

When he arrived, he found scores of women scattered in small groups in the lobby of the building. They wore shorts and blue jeans and pants suits. Some had their hair in curlers and wore no makeup and others were perfectly groomed and looked as if they were headed from the meeting to parties or dinner.

Suddenly, Trina Bellam appeared from a door behind a long table in the lobby. She was carrying an armful of papers, and

Mason stretched out his hands to help her. Thank God, he thought, breathing easier just knowing she was in his midst.

"No, no, it's all right. I can manage," she said, tugging at some of the stack which had gone astray in her rush. After setting the materials down on the table, she ran her hand though her short hair. "Whew, it's been a long day. Ready?" she asked Hank.

"I hope so." He was nervous, but he told himself that he could not afford that human frailty tonight. Bracing inside, he forgot about Hank Mason, the man, and clung to the image of a company president with one and only one objective—to get his fleet in the air again.

"We're going to start on time. But don't let the turnout bother you. We never get a full house." Her voice was low, and her eyes darted around the room. She seemed uneasy talking to him, as though she might be considered a traitor, he sensed.

"You don't have to stay here with me. Just show me where to sit and you're at your liberty," he said.

"Actually a committee was supposed to meet you with me. But look, I appreciate what you said. It isn't the best idea in the world to stand here talking to you like this. I'm glad you understand."

Trina turned to the girl beside her at the table. "Watch these papers, okay?" she said. Then Trina led Mason into the hall, a bare white room with gray metal folding chairs and a front table covered with a badly wrinkled green cloth. Mason seated himself behind the table and poured himself a drink of water from a clear plastic pitcher. Trina paused at his side and leaned on the back of a chair near his. "I hope everything goes all right. We have the police outside and a few guards around. It's just routine when a strike is on, so don't get worried when you see them."

"I'm glad you told me. I've never been to a union hall or to a union meeting in my entire life."

"It may not be all that you've seen in the movies," she said and smiled, brushing a stray hair off her forehead.

A female union official called the meeting to order five minutes later and introduced Mason. There were a couple of boos and few scattered claps from the audience that Hank imagined to be about two hundred women and a handful of men.

They appeared to Mason to be a gangling class of college freshmen, most of them young and fresh-faced, lively and chattering as he tried to speak. As he told them of how he started the airline business and where the industry was today, they seemed to grow serious, to be listening to him. He heard the sound of his own voice making an impact upon them and he could feel an increasing rapport with the members. These were his people in effect. They were all part of the same company, a family of people trying to make something live, survive. The room was silent now except for Hank Mason's words.

"In short," he said, "perhaps I *have* neglected you and your contract, letting it sit without action. For that I apologize and I hope you'll give me another chance. I am simply asking for a better climate between us in the negotiating room and you, all of you—although you are not in that room—can help create a healthy atmosphere. Let us all negotiate in the finest spirit of free bargaining in a free marketplace." He stopped. "Hell, I want this strike ended. I don't sleep at night."

There was laughter and one girl shouted, "Yeah," and there was more laughter.

He went on, "I know many of our employees have spent many sleepless nights, too, worrying about how they're going to keep roofs over their heads. When is this damn thing ever going to end. I pledge you the support of the airline's labor attorneys and my own personal interest and support. We will try to arrive at a settlement that you can live with. No, tonight I haven't come here to offer specifics but only to say we need you, we will try harder, and we will not neglect your needs or the needs of the union again. Thank you."

There was light applause at first and then it grew, and a few girls stood and cheered. Most of the audience followed in their show of approval of Mason's message by clapping.

The union official who had charge of the meeting asked if anyone had a question for Hank Mason, and there were a few hands raised.

A girl wearing a tight T-shirt with "Airways" stamped on it jumped to her feet. "Does this mean you're going to allow women to fly as long as they want? Not farm 'em out as soon as they get crow's feet?" she shouted.

"I do promise to take a new look at the female flight attendants' long-term career goals. Yes," Mason said.

"And what about making us look like prostitutes in those stupid uniforms? What about that?" an older flight attendant, who wore a well-cut pants suit, questioned him.

"The union and the airline will choose uniforms together. I think that ought to produce more acceptable dress, don't you?" Mason answered.

The girl nodded in agreement.

After a few more questions, the crowd began to disperse, with some members drifting out of the room before the meeting was ended by the chair. Despite the progress Mason felt he had made, no individual stopped to say he'd done a good job. There was still the silent pressure between them, labor and management. Perhaps no member wanted to be seen talking to the other side. Even Trina did not come to his side but left the table and made her way through the clumps of people to the lobby. Finally, Mason left his place to find Trina. She lingered, talking to a man designated by the tag he wore as a union official from Washington.

When he left, Trina walked slowly over to Mason.

"Well, I think you've accomplished what you came for. We're offering to start negotiations again in Washington in two days if we can arrange for the national mediator to join us, and that's usually not a big problem," Trina said.

"Thanks," Mason said, and he held out his hand to her.

"I guess then we'll see," she looked away after shaking his hand.

The lights were turned off, and she said good-bye to a group of members leaving the hall.

"Can I buy you a drink?" he said.

"I don't think it's a good idea for us to be seen together," she said. "I know you understand. Maybe another time. I've got some homework to do anyway for the meetings."

"I know a place where nobody will see us, and you can drive in your own car."

"I don't know." She hesitated, looking around the lobby.

"Trina, this is harmless. Just a drink. I need to unwind. Maybe you do, too. The airline has a suite at the Bridge Inn. If you decide to join me, it's 1016. No one will see you."

He waited at the Airways suite at the inn for an hour, sipping a Scotch in front of the large window facing the field, watching the jets take off and land. His thoughts were aimless for a while—he was lost in the maze of blue and red lights that dotted the strips. It began to rain, a mist clouding over the window. The lights were diffused drops of color claimed by night.

After two drinks he decided Trina was not coming. And why was that so important to him, he asked himself. She had made it possible to carry out his plan, and even if only a relatively few members were there, the report of his visit would be carried in the union strike news sheet that was sent to every member. His reception had been decent, and it would take time to feel the reverberations of his going to the mountain.

If it was a girl he needed, there was Francine, and in a couple of days he could have Ashley again. Why did he need to see Trina? Still, he felt let down; perhaps, he thought, it's just that the mission is over. I have jumped a kind of hurdle…and then maybe I have jumped nothing at all.

Routinely, the next morning, Mason called Good Samaritan

Hospital. No, he was told by the head nurse on Lenoir's floor, there was no turn for the worse. Instead, Mrs. Mason's condition was described as good, but she still had to remain in the hospital until the doctors felt she was strong enough to leave. Time is just dragging on, Mason thought. But there was nothing he could do to speed up her recovery.

"Let me know the minute anything bad or good happens. My secretary always knows where to reach me," he told the nurse.

"Damn. Damn." Mason pounded his fist on his office table. Maybe he did need New York and a change. He felt he was a prisoner in his own limbo.

When Whitefield brought in the 14-page contract for the sale of the two jets to the Arabs, Mason did feel like taking an exit. "To face this daily demise, it's the worst way to live." He frowned at Whitefield who seemed to Mason to ignore his comments.

"Just read this and sign it and let's get this off to Broderick in New York," Whitefield said. "Have your wife's attorneys bothered you again?"

"I don't return their calls."

Whitefield scratched his balding head. "Is she better?"

"Yes, more or less. They still won't say when she's coming out. I should bring over my own surgeon from New Orleans."

"Speaking of that fair city, you remember our buyers want the planes there, and they want you to be there, too. There will be picture taking, press releases, you know, the usual ritual that goes along with plane selling. They are also setting up a luncheon and dinner at Antoine's and Moran's, respectively. It's a command performance, I'm afraid."

"That's pure shit. I may have to sell them my planes. I don't have to bull crap with them over it. Never. Broadcast that I'm selling my planes? Write into this contact that there will be no news releases unless I see them first and no pictures of me released at all. That's the highest, damnedest kind of insult—to me and Airways right now."

Whitefield looked at Mason and then back at the contract on the table. "How did your meeting with the union go last night?"

"Who knows? They applauded. Some of them did. But who knows?"

"What did the union leaders say?"

"They're setting up new meetings in Washington in a few days, so I guess what I said could have helped. I don't know at this point."

"Well, we may not have to sell the whole fleet after all. By the way, did you authorize an Ashley Channing to do a new advertising campaign for us? The people in marketing are rather flustered by her lunching with the veep, who's in the dark, too. That kind of politicking between an agency and a company can cause a great deal of talk and friction."

"I didn't authorize anything. She came to me and I sent her to marketing, set the lunch up, in fact."

"Well, she's going ahead and doing a whole presentation and that is because marketing thought you picked her. Hank, maybe you should tell them and stop her from…"

"There's no cost to us in that kind of presentation. I signed nothing. Besides she's…she's quite a woman."

"I see," said Whitefield. "I understand completely. I will tell our marketing vice president before he has a coronary."

"It's not exactly what you think. She does have some good points. Let her submit her ideas. We're not married to any agency. I'll have this contract back to you by noon."

When Mason finished reviewing the document, he tried to reach Trina at the union hall and then at the second number printed on her card. There was no answer. Soon he knew why.

Mid-City Hospital, several miles west of Miami International Airport, called him to tell him a Miss Trina Bellam was asking to speak to him. The nurse said Miss Bellam had been injured in a car accident the night before. Then he heard a nervous, shaky voice. It was Trina.

"This isn't your problem, Hank, but I do need to see you. I'm…I'm nervous about some things."

There was an awful pleading in her voice, Mason thought. Strange feelings about her car accident crept into his head. "What kind of accident did you have? How badly are you hurt?"

"Cuts and bruises. Nothing that will keep me down for long."

"I'll be right there," he said. The contract would have to wait.

In 20 minutes, he was by Trina's side in her private room. Her description of her condition was underplayed. Her face and her legs were patchworks of bandages and tape. "How did this happen?" he asked.

"I don't know exactly. I was leaving the union meeting, and a car hit mine. That wasn't the worst part. I don't know if I should go into all this…" she stopped. "It's awful." She started to cry.

"Trina, somebody did this to you intentionally. You might have been killed."

"The bruises and the cuts came after the accident," she said, looking away from him. "But the police don't know that."

"They'll find out if they don't know already. Did you know any of these people?"

"No, they were masked, wore stockings over their heads, women and men. They said I was getting a working over for two-timing them."

"Then I'm responsible for this? Oh, God, you're getting protection before I leave this hospital. And the police have got to be told. Everything you know."

"They didn't believe all this happened in the car accident so they're probably investigating, although I won't tell them anything. I can't. Hank, you might be in trouble, even danger. I don't know who these people are. They may be much bigger than our local union or even our big union. You just can't get involved."

"Did they say anything else, Trina?"

"No." She held her face for a moment with both hands as if she was in severe pain. "They said I wouldn't be able to hold my job in the union anymore. And if I tried there wouldn't be another practice session. They said I was in a conspiracy, that I was getting some pay-off from you."

"God, I'm sorry. You have to know that, and you have to know that I will stand by you come hell or high water. You'll have to trust me. Don't worry about money. I'll see that everything is taken care of."

Trina was crying again. "Just go now. I just can't talk anymore."

Her doctors had told Trina she had sustained lacerations and fractures and would be under their care in the hospital for at least ten days more.

Recalling the threatening phone call at his office, he knew he should have listened, and he should never have gone to the meeting. Now Trina would be out of the negotiations entirely and would be ousted from her union leadership. Somebody was out to show Mason he'd better stop tampering with the union process and power.

Back at his office, Mason arranged for guards to be stationed outside Trina's hospital room, and they would be further assigned to her when she was released from the hospital and sent home.

His labor attorneys in the capital told Mason the union had asked them to resume talks and that the federal mediator had said yes to any place any time. Mason could not reconcile the union's positive action with the brutality its members had probably committed on their own leader. Unless, he thought, these were extremist members or some strange union sympathizers. Who could be sure of who they were and what their motives might be. Maybe he should stay out of the picture. No, that would be defeat. There was Trina to think of. Well, they had already gotten to her and now, with the protection he'd arranged, he had to take the chance.

"I want to be there at all the talks," Mason told one of the young lawyers who was working in Washington for him. Mason knew by his tone of voice he did not approve, but Mason was his boss and wrong or right, a boss cannot be stopped.

Before he left for New York, Hank worked feverishly to get his desk cleared of pending matters—especially the signing of the contract for the sale of the two jets to the Arabs. It was painful, but it had to be done. And then he went to see Lenoir at the hospital, who appeared to be recuperating.

"I don't know why you keep coming to see me," she said when her husband appeared at the door. "Is it guilt or are you waiting for my money?"

Despite what the medical report was, Lenoir appeared pale and languid to Mason. "I sure as hell don't want your damn money, Lenoir. What about Everett? Have you heard from him?"

"He's coming home very soon. Thanks for having a secretary track him down." She pulled a cigarette from a pack under her pillow. "I'm not supposed to do this but I have little else. I can't get my hands on any booze."

Leaning back against the raised head of her bed, she blew smoke in Mason's direction. "How's your union problem? I've been reading about the long delays. I suppose, Hank, all your sins have come back to haunt you."

"I didn't know hard work was a sin."

"I don't mean the work, my darling. I mean all your fast living, the total amorality of Hank Mason."

"Since when were you a moralist?"

"Basically, I am a believer in the Old Testament. I always have been. I do believe that evil is returned to the evildoer. An eye for an eye and all that."

"You lie there in a hospital bed, aching, and still have room in your mind for this kind of hating. I don't understand you, Lenoir."

"You don't understand yourself, Hank, much less anybody else. But I think I know you extremely well. It's a simple enough study. You fell in love with a rich girl and tried to make it on your own, which you did. But the girl's real need for you was ignored. You could have lived peacefully on her money. What is money anyway? And it really wasn't mine. I was an accident of birth like everyone else. Life for us could have been idyllic but…it's gone forever."

She put her head back on the pillow and began to look at a magazine that lay on her bed. "Thanks for coming by," she said without lifting her eyes from the pages.

As he left the hospital, he wondered why he had gone, why he kept running back to her. He was an adolescent about Lenoir, and he hated himself for not cutting off all ties to her. But who else was left to stand by her? No relatives, a son who ignored both of them. He had no one either. The women who drifted in and out of his life did not care about Hank Mason, the man, the human being. He was not fool enough to believe anything they may have said to him in flights of passion or gratitude.

Ashley Channing was more strikingly beautiful than Mason had remembered. She stood before the marble fireplace in his suite overlooking Central Park.

"This apartment used to belong to one of the world's richest and most colorful women. But she could never have done it more justice than you," he said.

"You do know how to flatter a girl, don't you? And your wife, does she own it now or you said your company…"

"My company owns it."

She moved gracefully from the fireplace to one of the large windows that faced Fifth Avenue and the park beyond. "It's quite elegant. I've always liked The Pierre."

Ashley belonged in this setting and in New York. There was that certain chic about her, Mason thought—the lines of the beige pants suit she wore, the simple gold earrings, the heirloom bangle bracelet, her hair loose, casual, but expertly cut. She embodied the finest packaging of the city, the same quality that Lenoir displayed when she wanted to.

"I've finished your presentation. Care about seeing it?" She paused. "Well, you will when your strike is settled and your service is resumed. Your marketing people can't possibly turn me down.

But I'll go through the corporate channels. How long are you staying in New York?"

"Long enough to have an affair with you."

She laughed. "Well, that will only take five minutes. I operate at a high pitch all the time."

"I'm not that speedy," he said, smiling.

"That's not my experience with you." She sat down on the long white sofa, running her hand over the silk upholstery.

"You have ties of any kind, Ashley?"

"Not real ones, superficial types. Hmm." She folded her arms and stared at him. "And you, do you have ties?"

"You know all about me." Her games were amusing as a change. He could not bring himself to be serious after what he had left behind in Florida. Here was a luscious woman who was making no real demand on him, who could bid him adieu with the same cool touch with which she could welcome him.

"We have lovely surroundings. We're young and healthy. So why not have a good time? Let's not get wordy. Okay?" She smiled.

Mason saw himself reflected in the woman who sat before him. There was nothing between them but the handsomeness of material things, the needs and desires of their bodies, and some moments of thrills. That was usually all he had with any woman. But lately there was that growing ache in the pit of his stomach, telling him he needed more than this. It was all birthday cake and there was no substance, nothing left after the bright moment of ecstasy.

"A good time. Is that what it is to you? To me?" He stared at the park multiple stories down. There it was, a canvas of brown with winter sludge and the grime of the city descended and ingrained in it. Some patches of dead grass were darker than others. The trees looked like twigs from where he stood, and the only life he could see were the skaters on the circle of white ice at the far end of the park. Was this the landscape of his life; was there a lesson for him in this picture? He felt the old Hank Mason tug at his sleeve. You're getting boring, he thought.

"Don't be snide about my life," she answered, "if you must about your own. I've worked hard to get where I am, to play when I want to. I'm not ashamed of any of it, Hank."

That was the first bit of seriousness he could remember hearing from Ashley, and he didn't know if he wanted that kind of behavior from her. "And I thought you were all icing."

"I'm blood and guts when I have to be. And when I work, I work. Like hell. And I have fun the same way. If you don't want to play, then I can find someone else," she said, reaching for her brown leather handbag on the sofa.

"I'm sorry, I didn't mean anything. I'm not in one of my better moods."

"I don't feel like a scene, and the vibrations between us at this moment are not happy."

"Again, I am sorry. I'm taking my hostilities, my troubles, out on you. And I have no right…"

"Save them for the proper people. What you need is a party. A friend of mine is giving one tonight and we'll go."

"Which friend is that?"

"It doesn't matter, does it? The guests will all be provocative and witty and glamorous. There won't be a bore there—at least after you've had a smoke or a drink or whatever you want—everybody will be just mellow."

Hank did his best to give her a convincing smile, and suggested they have something to eat first. She shrugged but led the way out of the apartment.

At dinner in the Oak Room of The Plaza, Ashley received three phone calls at their table. After the last call, the waiter left the phone by her side.

"Is this all business?"

"Some of it," she laughed. "My clients can get to me at any hour. For instance, that last one was president of Best Aspirin. I call him Frusby, an old family name I happened to pick up at a party from an old college pal of his. One of his ads on NBC *News Tonight* was cut a second short. When you're spending millions of dollars with a national network, pressure's got to be applied when they make a mistake. He watches every commercial, and I hear from him almost daily. Don't you watch your ads?"

"Well, we look at our ads, too, and somebody at my agency would have caught that slip-up."

Mason liked the liveliness in her voice as she talked about her business. There was a complete femininity about Ashley, although she did not possess the physical fragility of Lenoir. There was a real womanliness to Ashley. Sitting close to her in the black leather seat, he smelled her heavy, expensive perfume and it excited him. Her hair was silky smooth and cut in slight waves that framed her face. When she spoke on the phone there was a robust, healthy force in her tone.

In total, Ashley was a highly desirable woman—in business, the bedroom, anywhere, he decided. He felt special when he was with her, and he was glad to be lost in her aura, in her New York for the time being. It was pleasant to forget…and he could with her.

When the phone rang again, she answered it. "No," she handed the receiver to Mason, "this time it's for you."

There was an urgency in Whitefield's voice that Mason did not like. Mason nodded his head, taking in what his colleague told him. The media in Miami had blown Trina's accident into front-page material, and the police were calling it an assault-and-battery case. They even suspected attempted murder. "So they think, both the police and the attorneys, that I should be at the meetings in Washington. Well, hell, regardless I would have been there anyway." Hank shook his head.

"Bad trouble, Ashley," Mason said when he hung up. "But there is nothing you or I can do about it. So tonight we're going to that party. I just want the pressure turned off for a while." He tried to convince himself that the heat could be lowered. But how? Attempted murder…the entire scene had grown to ugly, dangerous proportions. Be grateful, he told himself, that Trina is alive.

Chapter 8

Hank and Ashley went to the party in one of the hansom carriages parked across from The Plaza at Central Park. The clippity-clop of the old horse and the swaying of the buggy on the cold night made Mason smile. He put an arm around Ashley and pulled her to him.

When the driver stopped after a half dozen blocks up Fifth Avenue, Mason gave him a $100 bill and asked him to be back at the same spot at 1 a.m. and he would match the first payment. The driver took off his cap to his generous customer and waved good-bye. Mason and Ashley nodded to the doorman, and she announced herself and Mason as guests of Mr. Fennelley.

Their host's apartment was a penthouse of 30 rooms, Ashley told Mason. The living room air mingled with the scents of roses and tobacco and perfumes. Lost in the density were people so splendid and bizarre that Mason wanted to stand back and study the scene before him as he would have a painting. He had known assortments of characters, but they could never match this collection for variety.

Ashley led Mason through the thicket of humans who smoked and drank and smiled at the couple as they cut a path to Fennelley, who stood on the outer rim of a circle of guests. He was a short man with bead-like black eyes and a waxed mustache that stood out three inches on either side of his face. When he laughed, he showed large, sparkling white teeth. He drank from a tall, thin glass and when he saw Ashley, he turned from his friends and embraced her, burrowing his face in her breasts.

"Oh, God, when are you going to get that airline of yours off the ground, Mason?" he said when he was introduced to him by Ashley. "I adore flying Airways, and the girls," he said with a snicker. Then he turned with a quick gesture to Ashley. "I'll have a party on the yacht soon. Please come, Ashley, and give New York a rest, darling. And bring Hank Mason. He looks fun."

Ashley kissed the top of Fennelley's balding head, mussing the few strands of black hair he had left. Fennelley went back to his conversation, leaving Ashley and Mason on their own again.

"He's a real phony but lovable. He owns several companies we handle. But that's a bore. Let's meet people." At that moment, Ashley was carried away from his side by two males who seemed, by the glaze over their eyes, to be in another world.

At the bar, Mason ordered a Scotch and stood near the massive windows which gave him a panoramic view of the crest of New York at night.

"Hey," a high-pitched voice startled Mason. "I work for you." A tall blonde girl stood in front of him. Her overly generous breasts were the size of melons, hugged together by a dress whose neckline was cut to her waist. A champagne glass wobbled in one hand and with the other she started patting Mason on the shoulder to emphasize her remark. "I think you are super, Hank Mason. Can I call you Hank?" Her eyelids were slow and lazy from the drink. "I'm a stewardess…flight attendant. I like to say stewardess. And you know what I hear?" She leaned toward him to whisper, spilling her drink on his coat sleeve. "That you're the best at what you do in Miami, no, the whole damn state. That's right." She giggled and slowly leaned back to regain her balance, or what remained of it. "And we all know what you do!"

Mason nodded and managed a half smile. "I'm glad to meet you." He disliked himself for being such a fraud, but he thought his bland courtesy would turn the girl off quickly.

"Well, you know who I'm with tonight? Senator T. Samuel Smithly. You know him. He said he knew you. He's somewhere here. A real doll. I met him on one of my trips to Washington. He's a super man. Five kids, and he still has time for all this politickin' and a wife, too. We're here fund raising."

As a male arm reached out of nowhere and guided the girl off,

Mason ordered another Scotch. He did not try to see to whom that arm belonged.

Not finding Ashley in the crunch of people that had swollen since they arrived, Mason did locate the stairs and used them to get to the second and third floors of the apartment. The middle floor was just as crowded—it had two bars—and on the third floor he found sets of lovers scattered among the furniture groupings. Some twosomes were male, some female.

"Hank," a voice cried out above the din of the crowd. "I'm over here." It was Ashley.

And he found her sitting on the floor in a circle sharing a cigarette being passed around. "Want some?" She smiled up at him.

"No."

"The party has just started, Hank. It gets rolling in about an hour." Ashley turned back to her group and then as he started to leave, she pulled his leg and he fell to the floor. She grabbed him and kissed him savagely.

He knew his face was crimson, but no one seemed to care or even notice what happened. "I think I better get out of here," he said.

"Oh, sure. I'll see you later at the hotel," Ashley said.

A part of him wanted to stay, to escape into this web of depravity. Another inner voice told him to leave. He floated about the rooms which appeared upholstered with stylishly dressed men and women, and a few people whose sex he was not sure of. There was a hint of music here and there and people danced in loose groups or individually. He might have been somewhere in space as easily as he was here. It was another planet and while he knew this was Ashley's regular routine, he could not get it on in the rooms of strangers like this. He started to find the front door when his left ribs were tickled by long, sharp fingernails. A slithery creature with waist-length, straight black hair and amber eyes made up heavily with green eye shadow and silver sequins put her arms around him.

"Going somewhere?" she said in a deep voice. "Reginald Fennelley said I should see that you have a good time tonight." The girl was rake thin with a flat chest, and her hip bones stuck out like pins in the shiny blue dress she wore. Her brown shoulders were bare, and the top of her dress was held up by a string of sapphires around her neck. Attaching herself to Mason, she hung on his every motion and when he tried to walk away, he felt the weight of her leaning on him.

He laughed. "Look, I was just leaving."

"You're not having a good time? Any friend of Ashley's is a friend of Reginald and me. We like our friends and we want to keep them happy."

Her eyes, too large and too expressive for his taste, stared into his. "All right, what did you have in mind?"

"Upstairs in the solarium. Reggie has a marvelous solarium." She clasped his hands and pulled him behind her through the crowded rooms and up to the third floor again. Through a door was another set of stairs and that led to a room which held a Plexiglas ball which filled half the enormous room. From outside of the ball, he could see orchids and roses and huge ferns. It was breathtaking. Inside the sphere were large, clear plastic chairs, small fountains spewing colored water, hanging baskets of gardenias and billowing vines.

The girl locked the door to the lush garden behind them. "Take everything off and let me give you a shower." She waited. "I mean it's like rain when I turn the showers on. And we can dance. Reggie calls it his rain forest bubble."

Mason laughed. In all his traveling, in all his conquests and pursuits, he had never had a shower in a Plexiglas bubble with a freak in the middle of an asphalt hell.

From the grass under his feet, and overhead from among the thickets of suspended foliage, came fine sprays of perfumed water. The girl massaged his head and told him to relax. The hours that followed fused into fantasy and back to reality only long enough for him to want to escape again into the dream world created by the homely, short man called Reginald and the nymph whose name he did not know.

Adrift in his own private world of sensuous pleasure and fulfillment, Mason returned by hansom to The Pierre. The next morning he did not remember coming back to the hotel or opening the door for Ashley in only his pajama top—which Ashley swore he did.

After a pot of coffee arrived by room service and she had a cup, Ashley sat up in bed. "I think you're a regular old Puritan at heart," she said. "That's refreshing. I never would have expected it from an airline person, especially not one with your reputation."

He laughed aloud, despite the pounding in his head, thinking about the entanglement with the girl in the bubble garden. "Were many of those people your friends?" he asked.

"Some. I do business with many of them. Artists, photographers, company presidents, models, designers. There were all kinds of people there. Reg has a real assortment of acquaintances."

"I noticed."

"Didn't you have a good time?"

Mason saw her reflection in the mirror opposite the bed—she was smiling to herself. She was gorgeous, and he looked and felt rotten. "Helluva time. You?"

"Always do. I am the supreme hedonist. I enjoy life. Every minute of it."

"I'm curious," he said, reaching for a robe from a nearby chair, "ever been married?"

"Once."

"And what happened?"

"It was a drudge and I was young, very young. I met a Texan in New York. I yearned to get back to the wide open spaces; but, well, when I arrived I saw what was really ahead, babies and bills and dust and tumbleweed and death and a tomb on the prairie." Her voice was low and sad.

"Then I'm sorry I asked."

"No, it's all over and now I have a life I made. A life I like. There isn't a deep, dark truth about me. You can see I don't brood. I live a day at a time. Work, sleep, eat, drink, and don't think too much. I guess that's my motto. You're much too serious. We're not here forever you know." Nude, she sprang from the bed and headed for the shower.

Shaking his head, Mason looked at his tired eyes in the mirror and rubbed his stubble of a beard. Why in heaven's name was he involved with somebody else? Well, he thought, it was a way of forgetting, if only for brief moments.

After two cups of coffee, Mason read the *New York Times*, and when he found a small item reporting the sale of his 747s to the Arab group, he called Whitefield. "What the hell, Whitefield. How did this happen?"

Whitefield explained that the buyers had only answered general queries from the press about rumors of Airways' sale of equipment. "I know it's bad for the market, but this is public information now."

"It might work in our favor after all. What do you think will run through the minds of the unions when they see our planes being sold off?"

"That's a point, Hank."

"Do me a favor. Find out how Trina Bellam is, and let me know, ASAP." He hung up, his mind racing with how the news of the sale would help him when he got to Washington.

Wrapped in a large yellow towel, Ashley stood in the bathroom doorway and smiled at Mason. "What are you in the mood for?"

"I want to ask you something. What do you do if you're courting a company run by a woman?" It was none of his business and he knew it.

"I make adjustments," she said. "A girl has to earn bread, doesn't she?"

They did not talk about his account until early afternoon following a lunch at the 21 Club where she was greeted by a dozen customers and by waiters who called her by name. But Ashley was undaunted and continued her pitch for his account. "I want to build you—the man, the creator of Airways—into a campaign. I want your public relations people to get you out to talk to people—all kinds of groups in your system cities. I can get you spots on the major talk shows. A book, your autobiography, should be released next year. I have a ghost writer in the agency."

"You sound as though you have stolen the account already."

"You mean you're not convinced I should have the account?" She glared at him.

"I told you a long time ago, Ashley, I wasn't the one who would decide."

"But you could if you wanted to. You are the boss and you do own considerable stock."

"That's not the way I run my operation. I told you that."

Ashley did not speak about the ad campaign as they walked toward Fifth Avenue in the direction of The Pierre. He put an arm around her and she drew close to him, and as he looked at her face, flushed against the cold wind whipping against them, he decided he would talk to the people in marketing about putting her ideas up for review in direct competition with the ads and plans the current agency was churning out for Airways.

On Sunday, Mason was alone in his apartment at The Pierre. He spent hours recapping the events which led to the strike, and then he plunged into a day-by-day account of the negotiations and stalemates Airways and the union had been through in the long shutdown. Vacillating between anger and regret for the mess both sides had made of their differences, he wished like hell Trina were going to be in Washington tomorrow—to build into her argument what he knew she felt was right. And that would have made the difference. He knew it would.

But he was just daydreaming. Trina was kicked out of the arena, and her going back to her spot on the negotiating team was dubious, at least for now. Mason stared at the stack of papers that sat before him on his desk. He stalked about the room with the misery of

Trina's condition, his wife's illness, the strike, the threat of losing his airline looming over him. Never had he doubted himself in quite this way. The bigger they are the harder they fall—he knew now what that cliché meant. Where would he go if he lost Airways? What airline would have him...and as what? An administrator? Head of maintenance? He knew every nut and rivet of his aircraft, every part of modern engines. He was sinking, allowing himself to think this way. There were other alternatives. Starting a new airline in South America—that wasn't so ridiculous. South America was a new frontier in this worn-out world. He had many Latin friends who had approached him to join them in air-shipping ventures between the Americas and to other distant world points.

A call from Good Samaritan brought him back to the moment. Lenoir had an infection from the operation, and the drugs they were using were not helping her, he was told. Her situation was not critical, but the doctor calling wanted Mason to know there were changes in her condition.

"What can I do? You know I can have any drug from any place on earth shipped immediately." Mason squeezed the middle of the receiver. "Damn it, what can I do?" He waited, trying to control his panic. He had known too many people to die from post-operative infections. "Yes, yes, I understand. I'll be in Florida tomorrow afternoon and my office knows where you can reach me in the morning."

Mason hurled the phone against the wall. What the doctor said echoed over and over in his head: "The worst part of her condition, Mr. Mason, is that she has no will to respond to any treatment. It seems she has lost her determination to live."

Chapter 9

New York's painted face sagged at daybreak, Mason thought as his spine bounced on the hard seat of the cab taking him to LaGuardia Airport to catch the shuttle flight to Washington. He watched the night people as they emerged into day. Waitresses, barmaids, musicians—all still in uniform.

And hookers wrapped in tired fox stoles. And bums with baggy pants and torn shoes looking for cigarettes and God knew what else along the gutters. And then a sign of newness and another day—street cleaners in their morning-fresh outfits trying to wash away the carnival of the night before.

Mason sighed as he watched the glut of humanity around him, some of it so close to the bottom side of life, but there they were. Surviving. Why couldn't Lenoir survive? She had known nothing but the top of life and all its glory.

Finally, they boarded the craft and were airborne. In his mind, all the way into Washington National Airport, he was with the pilot every time he touched an instrument or answered the tower and the air traffic controllers for instructions. Vicariously, he felt the yoke and saw the panel flashing red and green and blue. He could smell the closeness in the cockpit, the heat from the instrument panel, the plastic and foam rubber, and the cool sweat of the crew.

Moving into a descent over Washington, Mason thought for an instant he had put the wheels and wing landing flaps down himself. As the captain taxied the aircraft onto the runway and headed it toward the terminal, Mason shook his head trying to break his mechanical reactions to the operation of the plane.

One of Airways' executive secretaries was just inside the terminal to meet Mason, and she hurried along with him past the other passengers to a limousine that whisked him to a nondescript, gray

Labor Department building where the federal mediator had his office.

The mediator's round, fat face was wet with perspiration which he mopped away with a wadded-up handkerchief. He smiled at Mason and they shook hands. "You know, Mr. Mason, this is an unusual request and I am going along with it because of the length and complexity of this labor dispute."

Mason nodded his head in agreement as he listened to the stocky man with the florid face and quick, animated gestures. Mason surveyed the hallway where they stood—a group of Airways attorneys, to whom he nodded, huddled at one end of the room, and the men and women who Mason assumed were from the union were at the other end. "I won't take much more time," Mason said, looking the mediator squarely in his eyes. "I have to get back to Florida today. I do appreciate this time, and I hope this appearance will work in the positive."

"We'll see shortly, won't we?" the man said, shaking Mason's hand again and wiping his forehead.

Mason rose from his place in the middle of the long, rectangular table.

His small audience seemed disinterested as he surveyed them. The two women, union representatives, scanned what appeared to be typewritten memos. His attorneys looked in his direction, and the other members of the group were in deep whispered conversations. The room's plain white walls, the simple brown wood furniture, and the general bareness around him created a sterile atmosphere, Mason thought initially. Then vibrations of tenseness hit him.

He cleared his throat. "To say that I knew what I wanted to say here today would be a lie. Until this minute, I sincerely did not know what to say to you. But here goes."

Looking at his knuckles, he began slowly. "I came into this room furious and I guess I still am, a little. One of the union members who would normally have been here has been attacked and hospitalized, and I am angry about that. Principally, because I helped cause it. I went to her to try to help end this strike. She's paying the penalty for my faulty judgment. I used her and someone made her pay for that. I'm paying for it, too."

There was only the nodding of heads as he announced Trina's accident. Well, they all knew about it and whether or not the union planned it directly or attacked her, they would not admit to it. Maybe the union had nothing to do with the assault. He could not accuse anybody.

Moving from the table, Mason paced the perimeter of the room. "I suppose I am to blame for a lot of indignation that the union feels, and I want to go on record as apologizing and pledging that I will remedy my attitudes and those of our executives." Mason stopped and stood at the back of his chair. "Look, I believe in free bargaining and the rights of every union and every employee. What I am really here to say is that we want this strike to end. But more, we want to be on the same side, united.

"What we do here in this room is emotional, it is subjective, hinging on the way we feel today, the way we accept one another, your reaction to me. But the result of what we say and our inter-actions to one another will affect thousands of people out there. Children and wives and mothers and fathers. The animosity between us has to end and end soon. This is not a threat. Please believe me, I am not here to threaten but to lay facts on the table. Yes, we've had offers of mergers, and we've had trouble meeting our debts. We are selling aircraft to meet payroll and other expenses. It's as simple as that. Management pledges its full support to reach an agreement quickly. We will not give the airline away to do it, but I do offer my personal support. I promise that we will try not to furlough employees when we do get back to work, even if we have to work short shifts to keep that promise.

"I do not mean to take over negotiators' work. I just thought it was time I came to you, face to face, to see if we can settle our differences and get back to work."

A woman with short, dark hair raised her hand and Mason recognized her to speak.

"You realize, Mr. Mason, that our union did not begin our problems. Contractually, we were ignored while other unions, male dominated, were able to settle on wages and benefits quickly. You realize, too, that we are tired of being treated like second-class citizens. The attitude toward us seems to be that of a parent reacting only when the child screams. Well, we'll scream for as long as it takes…and another thing…"

Mason realized he was about to see the real lava erupt now.

"You, Mr. Mason, have used a number of the females of Airways as your private property and…"

One of the Airways attorneys jumped to his feet and pointed a finger at the woman. "Now see here, Ms. Pratt, this is not a morality trial. Mr. Mason has not violated any member of his airline's staff or anybody else. As for your choice of words, you'd better realize you're maligning females, in general, at Airways, and Mr. Mason in particular. Overall, do you understand it takes two willing people to carry on the kinds of activities you've suggested? I think we had better end this kind of personal attack!"

"Let her finish. Go on, Ms. Pratt," Mason said, sitting down.

The woman sat back in her chair and crossed her arms over her chest. "I think Mr. Mason understands what I've said."

"Perhaps I have been indiscreet and perhaps I have been immune to the way my actions have affected employees," Mason said, dropping his eyes to the table. "And perhaps my behavior has set a bad tone for the reactions of this particular union at this time in our history." He cleared his throat. "I can only say again that the action toward this union and all other unions, and employees, male and female, will be different. I won't belabor the point. If there is anything I can do to speed up negotiations, our company's attorneys will be in contact with me and I will return to this room if need be. I thank you for this time and for listening to me."

Mason shook hands with the mediator, who rose and walked with him to the door.

Mason felt naked, his worst side exposed. It was impossible now to lift any discussion with these people to proper levels. The air was emotionally charged, negative. He felt heavy, defeated.

"This is a rough bunch from the union. I am sorry about the outburst," the mediator said in hushed tones when they reached the hall.

Mason's face was red. "Forget it. I can take it."

The young lawyer who had defended him in the negotiating room came running after Mason and grabbed him by the shoulder, excusing them both from the mediator. "Mr. Mason, I want to talk to you. You were brave to go into that cave. And about the girl, well, it looks as though she wants to be a heroine, make a big name for herself. Telling you off is one way of proving her strength."

Mason put his hand on the man's arm. "I want you to get in there and give 'em hell," he smiled. "That girl doesn't bother me. What she says only points to some probable causes of our trouble. Now, go back in that room and help settle this damn mess, and don't screw around with stewardesses in the future, if you know what's good for you. See what can happen?"

The young man smiled, Mason imagined from relief and surprise.

On his way back to Florida on a 747 of one of Airways' chief competitors on the New York-to-Florida run, Mason thought about what the Pratt girl had said. She had guts to speak her mind. He had gotten the message loud and clear. Leaders of unions often had their hang-ups about power and they often had psychological problems, but regardless of the personal reasons why the leaders of the flight attendants' union lashed out against him, there was truth in their observations. He decided he would stay away from the bevy of girls he had always been happy to choose from. That included Francine. Then Mason thought about Lenoir, the vision of her separated from his problems, from the daily stresses of living.

She was alone now and sick and without any drive to fight back for any kind of life. He would never understand her. Never.

Three doctors met with Mason when he arrived at the hospital in West Palm Beach. Lenoir's condition, they said, was serious. She had told her nurses to let her die. Lenoir could have visitors the next morning. There was nothing he could do, they assured him, and he would be contacted during the night if her condition changed for the worse.

At his office, Mason found his secretary waiting for him. It was after five and he wished she had gone home to spare him the busy work of signing letters and attending to details. He was glad that she just handed him a list of messages and said good night without lingering.

Lenoir's attorneys had called three times, and he was pleased his secretary used the good judgment not to put them through to him in New York or Washington. They knew about Lenoir's steady decline and were making one last attempt to assure themselves of a fat fee for changing power of attorney to him. He crumpled their messages and threw them on the floor of his office and then answered his private line.

"Yes, she's worse," he told Whitefield. "The meeting? Who the hell knows what good or bad I did?" Mason reared back in his chair and put his feet on the table.

"You're sitting, Mason?" Whitefield said. "We have had two merger offers today, one from Trans-Globe and another from International Flight. Trans-Globe has also applied to the CAB for temporary authority to serve our routes between New York-Florida and Florida-California. It looks as if they may win if the strike goes on."

"Hell, I was afraid of that. But they can't go through the red tape in the time it may take to settle the strike."

"The CAB will move swiftly on this one. The White House is getting all kinds of pressure to either settle our strike or let another carrier provide the missing service. Our legal department has prepared the argument against the request, of course, but we may lose hands down on this one."

"I'll talk to our government affairs man in the morning. We need to make a stronger pitch to the White House, too. The strike's the whole key to this damn thing, Whitefield. I'll hear, later on tonight, how things went today after I left."

"Meanwhile our 747s are in New Orleans ready and waiting. The Arabs are releasing the official news of our agreement the day after tomorrow. Our public relations people are simultaneously issuing press releases," Whitefield said.

"Is there any way we can stall the final agreement?"

"The banks are all set to transfer the money to us in New York, so I doubt it."

"You know what this sale might do to Trans-Globe's case to get those routes? And how fast our stock will go down when we're in the news on both counts?"

"It's crossed my mind, Hank." Whitefield seemed glib to Mason.

"Well, see if you can hold up the finalities of the sale until the CAB makes a decision, and we have a chance to let the President know our thoughts. I may go to the White House myself on this, or talk to the Secretary of Labor."

"I'll do what I can to set things back, Hank, but I doubt I can stop the wheels now. Please let me know about Lenoir."

"Sure." Mason set the phone down gently. Trina. There was Trina to worry about, too. He called her room at the hospital. Her voice was cheerful, and he felt better just hearing her.

"They're still investigating, but I wish they'd stop," she said. "It's over and I'm finished with the union. If this is what happens, if this is the kind of viciousness that's brought out in people…" she hesitated. "But I think it's over. They've made their point. I'm punished properly, and I'm out of the action now and for good. I've heard from a friend of mine on the committee that your talk went fine, and they are down to the fine shavings of the contract."

"You know more than I do then. I'm glad to hear that kind of news."

"Well, I believe you may see a contract before too long. It may even go out for voting by members in a few days."

"You have that on any kind of authority?"

"A union lawyer friend—I'd say that's a good authority. Both sides are very close now on wages and retirement benefits. Dental and special health care programs are the stoppers now."

"I wish my lawyers could tell me as much as you have. When will you be released, Trina?"

"Maybe in another week. They're keeping me here to take out the stitches on my face. Other than that and a few black and blue spots, I'll be fine…"

Mason detected some unhappy tones in her voice, and they shouldn't be there now that she was going home. "Are you all right? I mean you sound down," he said.

"I'll be fine…"

"I think I'll come over," he said.

"Later, maybe later, okay?"

"Sure."

He pictured Trina as he first knew her, hoping she would look the same when her ordeal was over. But what if she didn't? How would he be able to make that up to her?

Francine was wearing a white pants suit when Mason met her at her place. She poured him a Scotch and chattered about the weather and the height of the waves that windy day.

"What's wrong? You're not the Francine I know."

She looked at him questioningly, her eyes wide and sad. "A girl can tell when something's wrong. You haven't stayed away from me this long since we've been seeing each other. There has to be another girl or something. You haven't called, and when you did it was to see about my mother. I mean I'm grateful, but things are different between us. It's not the strike either. I feel something in the air." She shrugged her shoulders. "I guess I must be one of those psychics, huh?"

Francine walked away from him and stood looking through the sliding glass doors into the twilight. "I knew it had to end sometime—it's been fun anyway." She started to cry.

"Francine, you've been a good friend...lover. I won't forget. I've made arrangements for you to stay here at least another year."

"You didn't have to do that."

"Bring your mother down here and let her enjoy the sun. Look Francine, it's not you. I'm the problem. I'm making a few changes in my life and one of them is to stop playing with other people's lives."

"You haven't played with mine. I wanted to be your girl. And I'm not sorry I was. No more tears," she said and she turned to him and kissed him on the mouth.

Mason took her in his arms and held her for a minute. She looked up at him. "One more time?" she said.

"One more time. I guess that wouldn't hurt anybody."

"Just tell me one thing," she said, pausing outside her bedroom. "Is she pretty...and better than me? Does she make love better than I do?"

He held her close to his chest, her short hair silky against his chin. "No, Francine, you're on the wrong track. It's not a girl. No one makes love better than you do. All you need is the right man to appreciate you. And you'll find him one of these days."

At 8 o'clock the next morning, Mason was at the hospital and learned that Lenoir's condition had worsened. When he saw her, she handed him a long white envelope. Lenoir was pale and her eyes were gray and lifeless. "I'm not going to make it, you see, I don't even want to." Lenoir closed her eyes. A nurse with a thermometer came into the room then.

When the nurse had left, Mason reached for Lenoir's hand. "You're a young and beautiful woman." Her hands felt cold to him, limp and dangling extensions of a body that had abandoned life. This was not the same woman he had married; instead, Lenoir was a stranger lost in suffering and despair. And why? Was he that much to blame, he asked himself as he tried to soothe her in what might be her last hours on earth.

"Get out of here now," she said in a low voice. "I mean it, get out of here." She did not look at him but closed her eyes and raised a hand to cover her face.

Mason left the room, walked down the wide corridor past the floor desk and to the doctor's lounge where he found two of Lenoir's physicians. They took him aside and shook their heads as they talked. "It's just a matter of time now," one of them said.

"Yes, we're sorry, Mr. Mason. Really sorry. There isn't too much time..." the other one said. Mason left them.

Hank sat behind the steering wheel of his MGB in the open parking lot facing the lake. His head swirled in pain as the sun beat down on his face. "God," he said aloud and buried his head in his hands. Leaning against the wheel, he began to sob. The welts of sorrow pulsed through his body so that he felt every nerve of his being. "What have I come to?" he said under his breath. "A wife I have destroyed and a crumbling airline, that is my life. All the work, all the sacrifice...it has brought me to this moment. Death and destruction."

Mechanically, he drove to see Trina. He told himself along the way he had no one else who would understand. She could not refuse to see him. She just couldn't.

When he sat down with Trina in a small medical library on the top floor of the hospital, he apologized for summoning her to the rendezvous. "I just think it best that no one know I'm here," he told her.

"Is there something wrong, Hank? You look, you look as though..."

"My wife is dying." His lips quivered as he spoke, and he bit at them with a fierceness that drew blood.

She reached for his hands and squeezed them. "Cry, just cry, if you feel like it." Tears came to her eyes as she watched him. He wept then, without restraint. When he dried his eyes with a hand-kerchief she gave him, he looked at her hands on his. The silence between them was soothing to his agonizing emotions, and soon he'd regained his control.

"You've got enough damn problems of your own. You don't need any more," he said, smiling ruefully. "Where are you going after this? You can't go back to your apartment and you can't go back to work right away."

"No, my folks live up near Jupiter. I'll go home, I guess, until I'm well and ready to work again."

"You want to go back on the line again?"

"Flying has been my life since I left high school. I don't want to do anything else. You don't think they'll keep me off now that I may be a scarface?"

"There won't be any scars, Trina, and even if there are, no one better try to stop you from flying."

"They tell me there won't be any scars but..." She looked away from him.

"What do the police say now about all this?"

"They think they know who did it. Some informers told the police names, everything."

"Are they being charged?"

"Yes, but I have to testify. And I won't. My life wouldn't be worth two cents at Airways or anywhere outside this hospital if I did."

"And that's justice in the United States today. The violated have been scared to death and so have the judges."

"I'm afraid that's about it. You're afraid, too. You ordered the guards outside my door."

"Then you've got to be cool for the next month or so. There won't be any problems with money. I'll see to that. You'll be on paid leave."

"No, I don't want charity. I got myself into this, Hank, and I can pull myself out again."

"Mr. Mason," a nurse at the door interrupted them, "there's an urgent call at the desk for you. I'm sorry to take you away."

Mason kissed Trina on the cheek. "I'll see you later. I want to talk again…about *your* life."

Chapter 10

Mason's voice fell when he realized it was Whitefield on the phone. "The hospital's calling me, or what?" he said before Whitefield had a chance to say more than hello.

"It's one of our 747s in New Orleans, Hank. It's been bombed. Blown up. Nothing is left. Some of our people are dead. They don't know how many. You better get over here…"

Mason dropped the phone and ran toward his car. He sped to the office, hearing the news of the explosion on his car radio. Two men were reported dead and several others were injured. Gripping the steering wheel, he was seized by terror and anger. "Goddamn," he shouted, "I'm in a cyclone." On top of everything else bombarding him, Mason could not accept the blow-up as part of reality. This was a non-stop nightmare…when could he wake up from it?

Whitefield was waiting for Mason when he got to his office. Airways officials were hovering in the hall outside the boardroom near the elevator, their faces mournful and waiting for some action from him, Mason knew. He nodded his head to them and motioned them into his office.

"I'm stunned, shocked." He plowed a hand through his hair and stood looking out a huge window. "Whitefield, give us everything they know about this."

"PR can do better than I can. Mr. Rovensky, why don't you capsulate everything for us?" Whitefield said.

Ed Rovensky, a large, heavy man in his mid-fifties, stood by the door of Mason's office. He read from a shorthand pad: "The explosion occurred this morning in New Orleans at 10 a.m. Central Time. The bomb, police believe, was planted last night. It exploded in the rear fuselage area, then ripped at the first-class section. A fire spread to the upper-level cockpit. Two of our supervisory maintenance men were killed instantly. They were in the rear of the plane.

The names have not been released yet, pending notification of the families. The two others who were near the aircraft, supervisory catering personnel who had cleaning detail, are in serious condition at Ochsner Hospital." He added, "It's a wonder they're alive at all, I'm told."

"I'll go myself to see the families of all these people. I want everything done for the families. Everything. I'll be in touch by phone, Whitefield. I need to be in New Orleans."

"Hank, you're needed here. The Federal Aviation Administration, the National Transportation Safety Board are in charge now. Rovensky has the duty of going over to the scene of an accident along with the vice president of flight operations," Whitefield said.

"I don't care what the hell the procedure is. I'll be on a flight as soon as I can. Go on, Rovensky, what else? What else do they know?"

"They suspect it's a terrorist group acting against the sale of equipment to the Arabs. That's the tip they've been given."

"What about damage to the airport? Where's the other 747?" Mason said.

"Oddly enough, only one of the waiting rooms, ours, was damaged, mostly the exterior. No one was hurt inside since there were no passengers and no employees nearby. Seems these people are masters of explosives and know how to contain a blast. The other 747—thank God—was on the other side of the field, parked there temporarily until there was room for it on our apron area," Rovensky said.

"We may need all of you to man the phones in my office and in PR and elsewhere. Rovensky, would you agree? So stay put, everybody. I guess Rovensky and Whitefield will be in New Orleans on the scene later, a little later than I will," Mason said.

Rovensky nodded his head in sanction. "Yes, we'll draft a statement that everybody can use when questioned before we leave. Hank, how do you want to be quoted?"

"Say the company is deeply saddened by this act of sick violence which has destroyed human life. We offer sympathies to the families of our employees. We are perplexed; bewildered…you put in all the right words, Ed. I don't need to see it. Just go with it. Besides, I won't be around here much longer." Mason turned to Whitefield who had picked up Mason's private line. The group in Mason's office dispersed and followed Rovensky out.

"It's our Arab friends, Hank. They're screaming and they want a new contract. They may not take the one 747 without the other one," Whitefield said, holding a hand over the phone as he spoke.

"Shit! Get a new contract. And what about our insurance? Any way we're covered for an act of terrorism?"

"When the policy was written, terrorism wasn't even considered. Our attorneys will have to comb the clauses and see where there's a possible application. Meantime, Hank, we've got to talk about payroll. We can't meet it now, and we can't meet the notes on those planes," Whitefield said.

Mason fell back in his chair and covered his eyes with both hands. The blackness dizzied him, and inside, down to his lowest bowel, he was sick. But he told himself he had to get out there and fight like hell as he had never fought before. His body was numbed as he left his chair and stood with both hands clutching the side of his table. Sharp pains struck his leg. "Get out a letter, Whitefield, telling it like it is to all management personnel. I'll have to ask a small nucleus to stay, but it looks like a furlough for most managers."

"Of course, Hank. Anything else?"

"The people have to know the trouble we're in now. See if we can get by without interest on the plane loan. Under the circumstances…what can the bank do with ashes?"

The wreckage of the Airways 747 made a black charred junkyard of its own facing Airways' concourse of holding rooms which looked out over the landing field.

Mason stood in one of Airways' plush, first-class passenger

lounges and stared at the dead plane some 300 yards away. It was as if the plane had been slaughtered, mutilated by some mad, fire-tongued beast. Walking around the remains of the aircraft were gray-suited FBI agents and federal investigators who filled out forms they carried on clipboards. New Orleans police officers were there to assist, their cars pulled up on the apron heading in toward the wreckage.

The chief investigator of the National Transportation Safety Board stood in the lounge by Mason drinking coffee from a white china cup. "Helluva note ," the man said.

Mason looked ahead, oblivious to everything but the bizarre picture before him.

"It's getting to the point we're going to have to put airports off limits to everybody except bona fide passengers and look at how they're searched today. You know how much of a fight we'll have to put up in Congress to get funds appropriated for more security?"

Mason did not answer the man but nodded and went outside. A group of photographers streamed out of a nearby door onto the field when Mason made his exit.

Some of them tilted their cameras and bent down on hands and knees to get unusual angle shots. The mess before them resembled jagged peaks of a mountain range. And the sight of it all made Mason feel that he was surely not witnessing reality.

Airways had only two fatal crashes in its history, and in recent years its airline safety record was one of the best in the industry. And now this. How many people would not fly Airways ever again because of this insanity? He had already ordered that the other 747 be flown back to Florida—just in case the bombers were still around. But was there any real way of protecting his planes and people from the horrors that seemed to rule the world these days.

"You're Hank Mason, aren't you, president of the airline?" a young photographer asked him.

"At this point, who knows? But don't quote me on that."

"Can I get a shot of you with that in the background?"

"What the hell? Sure," Mason said, "Although I can't see why. It's our plane, or was, but beyond that this is a story of why—the government plays the big part now. Any questions should go through our PR people or the NTSB."

"Sure, the reporters will get to all that. I need a great shot to go with this big story." The photographer darted around like some nervous animal grabbing for a kind of kill.

Later in the day, Mason met with Rovensky and Whitefield in the lounge where the airline's press desk had been set up. They had flown over to New Orleans on a small, chartered plane.

"I don't want the names of the deceased announced to the press for two hours yet. That will give me enough time to talk to the families. I need a car and a driver right away." Mason explained he did not want to intrude on the family members, but he felt he had to say something personal to them before they were swallowed up by the media.

At dusk, Mason wandered alone in the French Quarter, losing himself among the tourists who meandered along the narrow sidewalks. He watched them gawk into the courtyards that led off the main streets. Despite the many times he had come here, he, like many of these people, found the novelty shops and art galleries tucked away in the courtyards intriguing.

Even at this hour, the night was coming alive with the smells of spices and coffee and French and Creole cooking floating out into the streets from the old buildings sandwiched together and leaning a bit from age.

The best of the Quarter was upon him. He heard the sounds of trumpets and the clank of cocktail glasses and beer mugs. The aromas of Bourbon Street—buttered popcorn, grilled hot dogs, fried onions—made him hungry. The barkers, mustached and wearing T-shirts with soiled satin vests, shouted out to passersby, tempting them to see the nude female bosoms pumped up with silicone. Inside the bars, Mason glimpsed the swinging breasts and grinding butts that surely were driving men crazy as they sat on their bar stools.

The night places rang—with jazz played on old, clunky pianos; with gospels sung by heavy-throated black women; with rounded, mellowed tones of brass horns blown by bearded, young white men and fat old blacks. There was the ring and bang of ragtime from banjos and from the tapping shoes of skinny black boys in the streets as they danced for coins flung at them by the crowds.

The sounds, the smells, the sights of this street of cheap, sensual ecstasy oozed through his body and his mind, and he felt at one with this place. He wanted to wallow in the carnival. He was already feeling half freak in this sideshow of life.

The faces of the families Mason had seen earlier were there in his mind's eye, etched sharply whether he wanted to remember them or not. Wives, husbands, children, parents of the women who were hurt and the men who had died on his plane—they had sat mournfully before him. There was that vagueness to their speech as if they were not really sure the tragedy had happened, as if they might be expecting their loved ones home for supper. Their shock was his, too, for he could not believe the horror of the bombing, of the deaths, of the injuries, of this senseless crime. At this moment, he could not comprehend the collection of his own troubles. They were too many to carry. How can this much go wrong, he asked himself. And yet he had no right, no right at all to indulge himself in self-pity.

I must be a kind of demon, or the devil must be covering my every step, he mumbled under his breath as he made his way to the Royal Orleans Hotel.

The potted yellow mums, the marble lobby, the gold-framed mirrors, the heavy crystal chandeliers lifted him for a moment. Doormen and desk clerks greeted Mason by name. In the lounge, which opened onto the lobby of the hotel, he ordered Scotch and a copy of the *New Orleans Times-Picayune*. When he tired of reading about the bombing and had drunk enough to feel numb, he rose and went out to Antoine's, just up the street. He entered through an alley door, the one used by old-time or regular customers. Inside he asked for Ray, the waiter who had served him here for many years.

Mason wanted to call about Lenoir, but he could not bring himself to hear any more sadness today. As he ate and drank some of the best food and wine New Orleans had to offer, he felt the complete hedonist. Why not? He raised a glass of white wine to himself. I've got one damnable life, he thought. My flesh will one day be rubble, too. And underneath the veneer of his actions, which he knew were shallow and temporary, he began to hurt, the pain and depth of his thoughts too much for him to handle.

Then later, in the streets, now crowded with humans scrambling for their pleasure, Mason longed to be with someone, to feel in touch with another human being, to get lost as these people were lost in their varying degrees of search.

"Georgiana on Toulouse," he said to himself as he walked up St. Louis to Bourbon, turning onto Toulouse to visit the house he frequented when he was in this city. The memory of Georgiana, the finest Creole blend of French and Spanish blood, swept over him and warmed his body. As he rang the bell at the black-lacquered door in the courtyard, he was glad to be here and to see the feminine vision before him.

The light on the woman's face was dim and soft. "Yes," she said. "Well, my God. It's Hank Mason. Come right in." She swung the door open wide and kissed him on the mouth. Her kiss tasted of perfume and wine, a combination Mason welcomed.

"How have you been? Oh, bad, I imagine. Real bad. I heard about the awful thing at the airport. Sit down and get relaxed," she said. She sat in a small, French period chair and smiled at Hank, and he felt a great comfort as he settled into the large, wingback chair near her.

"Some Scotch. How about that?" she asked.

"No," he shook his head. "Just to see you again and be here. I am tired."

"Yes, yes, my darlin', I know you are." Georgiana tilted her head to one side, her raven hair resting on her bare, tanned shoulders. He liked the sight of her, the womanliness of her, the manner she used to make him feel at home. There were no real questions about the past or about the future from her. There was a splendor to escape to in this house, so old and still. In a while, they went to her room upstairs. They lay whispering and laughing and making love until he had forgotten the misery of his day.

"Picking up the pieces and finding out the why is going to take a lot of time, Hank," Rovensky told Mason at the airport the next morning. "There isn't a lot of good we can do. The FAA, NTSB, and police are handling everything now. I guess you're eager to get out of here."

"Yes, I am. If there is anything I can do, Ed, call me at the office."

"I'll be back myself tomorrow," Rovensky said, shuffling a stack of press releases and trying to organize the long table which was in disarray with phones, typewriters, portable TV sets, and many used paper coffee cups. Mason used one of the phones to call West Palm Beach, and as he waited for a report on Lenoir, his hands began to shake. He lighted a cigarette and jammed it into the ashtray when he heard a voice on the other end of the line.

"Yes, yes, I'm her husband." His eyes fell on the table, although he did not see any of the objects in his view.

"Nothing. There is nothing you can do," he repeated woodenly. "She can't be moved. Yes, yes, I understand. My son, yes, please let me talk with him." Mason folded his arms and paused, his eyes searching the room. "Everett, you're all right. I'll be home this afternoon, and I'll come straight to you and your mother."

There was a coldness in his son's voice, and why not? They had not seen each other in more than a year and they had never taken the time to know each other. And now Lenoir's illness and imminent death were bringing them together. There had been a few happy times between them and now... Hank hung up the phone wearily.

"I'm swamped with requests for interviews with you, Hank. Any chance?" Rovensky asked.

"No. I can't give them anything really. All the facts and numbers speak for themselves." Leaving Rovensky, he walked to the expanse of windows of the lounge. Cranes and bulldozers picked and rammed at the scattered carcass of the plane. In hours, only a few scars and memories of the explosion would remain, Mason thought. Yesterday's sensation, forgotten headlines.

"There is some good news, Hank. The union contract looks as if it might be in final draft by tomorrow morning. That means a possible mailing to members by the end of the week and a counting of the ballots in another week at the most," Rovensky said.

"You think they're really that close? I've heard this song before."

"The lawyers say the mood of the group has changed drastically since the bombing. One of them said they want the union out from under suspicion."

"The powers that be don't suspect the union."

"They suspect a lot of people now, but they're not telling us, or anybody, anything official. They've had some tips from anti-Arab groups, terrorists groups. A couple of people have named the union. I personally don't believe it's the union."

"Well, we're not the police. And I've got enough worries without trying to solve the case. I'm concerned now with having enough security to see we don't lose any more planes or people. We've doubled the guards at terminals where our aircraft are mothballed. I'd rather nobody make any statement about that. It might just tempt some loon out there."

"Sure," Rovensky said.

Lenoir Mason died in her sleep. She had not been in pain, two of her physicians told Hank when he arrived at the hospital.

Everett stood behind the men, his long arms folded. He swayed in place as the three talked and watched Mason's face as he was told the details of her last hours.

Mason did not cry. He felt only an emptiness, as if part of his life had been washed away. His reactions after the initial news were nods and handshakes. He left the hospital with Everett, who did not speak until they stood in the front parking lot.

"Well, I suppose it's a kind of freedom for everybody," Everett said. The sun caused him to squint his small green eyes. He was a head taller than Mason, but his body was a reed, flexible and gangly. In the wind that came off the lake in front of them, Everett's blond hair blew off his face, and Mason noticed his paleness and the non-expression in his eyes.

But he sensed that this young man, this stranger to him in many ways, wanted to talk to him, to somebody. "You want to come with me over there?" Mason nodded his head in the direction of Palm Beach.

"I guess so. I don't have a place to go right now. I just got here. I don't especially want to go to her house."

Everett talked as if Lenoir were some distant relative the boy had hardly known, Mason thought. But their relationship was not far removed from that, was it?

At his apartment on the island, Mason offered his son a drink, but he refused it.

"I've learned not to rely on anything. No stimulants, nothing."

"Glad to hear it." Mason stopped. "Well, where are we, sitting here with your mother dead?"

"Where have we been?"

"I don't know, Everett. I guess nowhere at all. But look, you're home and you saw her alive, didn't you?"

"Yes, I saw her. In that condition, there wasn't much I could say or do."

"As her son, there's going to be a lot of business for you to take care of. You'll be a rich man in your own right. Far richer than I will probably ever be."

"That's not important to me—how much money either one of us has."

"You might look at it in a different light if you didn't have any money."

"I might, but I don't need money the way I live."

"You won't live that way all your life, Everett. Not when you're my age."

"Maybe. I suppose I just don't hunger for things. My generation doesn't, not the way yours does."

"Everything comes and goes in cycles. Your children will be different, too."

"You're taking all this cool enough. Did she leave you some of her estate? I assume she did."

"I don't want it if she did. I never wanted that from your mother."

"I guess you're still worried about whether or not I'm your son, aren't you?"

"No. It wouldn't matter to me after all these years. You are legally...and you just are."

"But you're not sure..."

"Damn it, Everett, drop it." Mason's voice rose. He sprang from his chair. "I was never much of a father. Does it relieve you to think of me as a stranger? Can you excuse me that way? Well, don't do me the favor. Your mother never wanted you too close to me. But I can't use that as my excuse for failing you. She won her battle because I had another child—my company. She used you, too, to punish me for building my airline and neglecting her." His voice mellowed. "I won't pretend I didn't have plans for you. Every son is his father's clay until a certain time in the son's life and then the dreams are all over. I'd like to think you wanted to come into the airline business with me."

"You never said that before."

"I never thought you'd listen to me. What are your plans now?"

"I'll go back to school. I may go into medical research."

"No plans for business?"

"It's not my track, Dad."

"If it isn't, it isn't. Just as I couldn't be a farmer like my dad. I understand."

Mason saw the boy's eyes fill with tears. Everett looked away from his father.

"If you want to cry, what the hell, cry," Mason said, pacing the room, wanting to reach out to his son. It was the first time he could remember Everett showing any emotion in his presence.

The boy sobbed, and it was the kind of cry that hurt deep inside him, Mason knew. The room was quiet, and Everett got up and stood at the balcony overlooking the ocean. "She's going to sea, you know. Her ashes."

"I remember she wrote that in her first will," Mason said. "Who knows how many times she may have changed it?"

"She told me a long time ago about that. And that she wanted only a memorial service for us alone, and the servants. Then a boat will take her ashes out there…" He sighed. "I suppose I *will* go to the house. I want to talk to Mary. And then just be alone," the boy said.

"If you need me, you know where I am," Mason said.

"Sure, we'll talk tomorrow."

When his son left, Mason remembered the envelope Lenoir had handed him the previous morning and pulled the unopened letter from the pocket of his jacket.

Hank,

I trust you will not have opened this until my death. I hope not. I am relieved now, remember this. I have lived in pain for so long that I am truly at peace, released from this holocaust called my life. You lived with my decadence, and you could not help me as I could not help you in any way. Yes, I loved you until the last breath of my life, but I could not live as part of your life because I wanted more intensity than you knew. The lust you wade in—that is a quagmire. I wanted surging rivers and rushing waterfalls.

One day you may learn about the kind of mountainous love I had to give—you may even feel it for someone else.

I believe we were destructive to each other because we stood blocking each other's way. If we had only grasped for mutual goals the world would have been shaken. But it is all too late.

Be good to your son now. You are all he has. And be successful with your company—because it is all you have and may ever have.

I have only two requests of you in this death bed. Know that I did love you. There was never any soul I touched as I believe I touched yours. Once.

And remember the possibility of love, not the kind you believe you had for me, but real love.

Lenoir

His hands trembled and the letter fell to the floor.

Chapter 11

The strike was still not settled. Several clauses were voted down in the contract that was mailed to all the members after the 747 disaster and that shot the entire document to the wind. There were more negotiations underway, and this time they were moved to Miami.

There was just no way of knowing how long a new contract would take to negotiate and rewrite. The rumor mill had it, said his labor attorneys, that there was a power play going on in the union, that members were being urged to reject the new contract sent to them in protest of current leadership. That might bring a new union regime forward. God knew what that meant in terms of new negotiations. Mason was as confused about the strike now as he was when it started.

As he drank coffee that Monday morning, he felt as if tankers filled with cement sat on his shoulders. He could not move or flex a muscle under the weight of his dilemmas. The only positive note that he could think of was the faith that showed in the airline and its future by his management employees. They had offered to stay on with reduced pay when he announced he would not be able to keep meeting their full payroll and hold on to capital. It was their confidence and the freezing of the loan demand since the destruction of the 747 that kept Mason alive now.

The Arabs were writing another contact and wanted two DC-10s instead of the lone 747, and these planes would be ferried to Europe. The Arabs also agreed that no report of the agreement would be spread to the press or any outsiders until the planes crossed the Atlantic. For that, Mason was grateful; although he knew somebody would leak the news to the aviation trades—and that it would be only a few minutes away from the wire services and then the world. He would just have to take his chances.

His phone rang and it was the desk downstairs. Ashley Channing, the clerk said, was here at The Breakers to see him. "Send her up, of course," Mason said. When he had replaced the phone, he wondered why he had given in so easily. There was nothing for them to discuss.

Ashley stood in the foyer of his apartment. She was dressed in a lemon yellow pants suit, her hair shone and her skin was fresh and taut. Extending her hand to him, she said, "I'm very, very sorry about your wife. You deserve a series of good things now and for a long time."

"Thank you, Ashley. I don't know why you're here. We really can't decide anything on advertising now. It's a waste of your time."

"I don't think so, Hank. Have you forgotten New York all that quickly?"

He looked at her, remembering. "Sit down. Breakfast? Coffee?"

"I've come for quite different reasons than what you may expect. First, to offer my sympathies in person…for everything. And to help end this silly strike."

"Oh?"

"Well, I have some contacts and I would have offered a while ago, but I just didn't think an awful lot about it. I want to know what you've tried—outside the negotiating room."

"The usual. Washington staff lobbyists. We've had a few Senators and Representatives write letters to the press and to the union about interruptions of service, even talk to some labor leaders. And we've gone to the White House. But, force against the union from the executive branch and the Labor Department has not worked. Maybe it's brought on deeper hostility."

"My approach is on the other side of the fence. I have a friend who is a lifelong champion of most of the labor unions. Through him, and a more subtle touch, that strike can be ended rather quickly."

"You think so?"

"I know so," she insisted.

"He must owe you a lot of favors."

"He does," she smiled. Gliding around the room, sure of herself, Mason noticed, she was in another world.

"Does that mean he's a lover? I thought you were too smart to get tangled up with Washington."

"Hank, we must admit somewhere along the line that those imbeciles in Washington do have power, if nothing else."

"Forgive my naïve spirit. Seriously, maybe we should just leave this friendship of yours alone."

"I am not indiscreet," she said as she nestled into a chair and crossed her legs. "I'll have some coffee now and a roll, if the offer still stands."

She reminded him of a smug, purring cat as she sipped her coffee. She had everything figured out, and he wondered if she really could deliver what she promised on the labor front. Well, what did he have to lose by letting her try?

"The papers in the East, mostly the tabloids, were not too kind in reporting your wife's death and your life with her."

"I don't want to see papers like that. People will always want to read filth."

"Oh, it wasn't all filth. It was rather exciting reading. People around New York are particularly curious about the dashing president of Airways. I may have some full-hour interviews on national talk shows—if my campaign is accepted. Soon, that is."

"I told you, Ashley, I've got more problems than you'd dream of, and ads don't interest me now. Why are you trying so hard with this account?"

"I have my reasons, Hank," she said in low tones. "A girl has to have big dreams in this business if she's going to survive. And I do have them and I will survive. At any rate, I want to get to know every facet of Airways so when you choose me, everything I do will be accurate."

"Be my guest. How do you plan to tackle getting to know Airways?"

"First, I'll walk through it all and do my own detailed story of the history of the company. Then I'll do an investigative report on each department. I'll know more about the airline than you do when I'm finished. Maybe a little more about you." She looked at the table where he had spread out papers from his office. "What are you working on?"

"My priority item is a statement on airport security and more airline security at airports—after what just happened to one of our planes."

"You don't miss a PR trick either, do you?

"It's no trick but if you want to read it that way…"

"I hear you have a son—where is he now?" She seemed to ignore his comment and was anxious to move on to other subjects.

"Here in Palm Beach."

"He must stand to inherit a great deal of money and art treasures and heaven knows what else. And you, you must have been named in the will—not that you need the money."

"We won't know for a while. I don't think I should count on anything. Not that I couldn't use it. But my son deserves most of it."

"I'll bet you're down to your last couple of million. What a pity."

"You haven't checked out my financial statement so well as you have my airline, Ashley."

"Oh," she said, sitting by him on the sofa. "Are things bad with you?"

"Let's say things are not good. I have to get back to work, Ashley."

"Will you have dinner with me tonight?"

"All right."

"If you want to work here at your suite, I could come by and pick you up. I've taken a house on the island, north end, for a little while."

"I'll be here."

When she left, he began to feel squeezed in by her conversation. He did not want to have dinner with her. It would be predictable— in spite of the excitement of her body and the surroundings. Trina was on his mind now, and she floated into his head at odd times and more often than he chose to admit. By this time, she would be at her parents' house in Jupiter, he reminded himself. And would she want to see him? He dialed the number she had given him.

No, Trina was not at home, a friendly woman told him after he introduced himself. She had gone for a drive with Doctor Jensen.

When he settled back to work at the table, Mason tried to keep his thoughts focused. He couldn't. His mind kept wandering back to the phone call to Trina's house and visions of Doctor Jensen. He was no doubt young and handsome and brilliant and most important—he was with Trina for a drive.

Mason called Trina several hours later and she answered. "I wondered how you were," he said. He was nervous as he spoke, and he asked himself why as he talked. "I mean you were with a doctor."

"Doctor Jensen is just a friend. I met him when I was in the hospital. He's a resident. He was there the night they brought me in. He's been wonderful to me. Helping me get the pieces back together again."

"I'm glad then…that you have him for a friend. Trina, I need to see you."

"Any time but….I thought with everything that's descended on you, you might want to be alone."

"Seeing you is the best medicine I could hope for. I'm alone when I'm with most other people."

"Tomorrow, why don't we make it tomorrow?"

"Yes, dinner. I'll drive to Jupiter and we'll have dinner up that way."

"I'd like that," she said.

Mason held the phone in his hand for a few minutes after she left the line. He felt like a teenager having asked for his first date.

There was not a man at Ta-boo on Worth Avenue who did not ogle at Ashley Channing as she entered the restaurant and bar on Hank Mason's arm. Throughout dinner, there were lingering glances at her from the men and women at other tables.

"I'm sorry you don't dance," she said after their liqueurs.

"With a bum leg like this, I'm afraid I'd only mess up your shoes."

"You're quite the enigma," she said, resting her face on clasped hands under her chin. "And one of the most exciting men I have ever known."

"You're not exactly the dullest woman I've ever met."

"Oh, you've known your share of thrills with women. I know about that, but I'm not interested in how I measure up. I'm only interested in us."

"Us or the account?"

"I'm looking for a permanent relationship, Hank. I may as well be that honest. Oh, I know that's not what I said in New York, but I've given it a lot of thought since then. I've changed my mind. I'm tired of the free-spirited life." She smiled. "There have been offers, but I haven't found the person I'd want to commit to."

"I imagine after what you're used to, Ashley, life with me would be a complete bore." Was this the same Ashley Channing he had known in New York? Or was this part of her plot?

"I don't mean that I'd devote my whole life to a man. I want a man who has a strong life of his own because I want my own world, too."

"You want everything, then."

"Yes, that's right. I want it all. Why not? Why not take all you can get from life? You have."

"No, I've only scratched the surface, and then I've done a *helluva* job with my life."

"Well, you fooled everyone around you. By the way, when can I start my study of Airways?"

"Tomorrow. I've told my executive vice president, Robert White-field, to meet with you and help you. He'll direct you anywhere you want to go."

"You won't be sorry about this, and you'll be firing your ad agency within a month. I'll deliver a campaign you can't turn down," she promised.

When they went to his apartment for more drinks, there was a message for Ashley to call Washington, which she did before she put her wrap and bag down. It was her friend, the Senator, and she laughed as they reminisced, sandwiching in bits and pieces of business.

"All right, darling, and thanks for everything. You're a love." She threw her bag across the room, and her white mink stole fell to her feet. She ran to Mason and grabbed him around the neck. "I told you, Hank. He's talked to the head of the big union that really calls the shots for the flight attendants' group, and that leader has laid the law down. They have a week to get this stupid strike over. I told, I told you." She kissed him hard on his lips.

"Wait a minute. Just like that?"

"I told you." She kissed him again. "I don't promise what I can't deliver."

"What kind of friend is this Senator?"

"We were once lovers, but he's married and can't get a divorce." She raced on, "You know the family image politicians have to have. But that doesn't matter. That's all over. We're good friends and we do each other favors from time to time."

Just like that, Mason thought. Some lovers. Some power. She had managed, or so it seemed, to stop a crisis that had crippled his airline and him for months. But he would have to wait and see. The whole thing could backfire. He could not be elated over what was still a promise.

"I feel like a swim in the ocean," she said, twirling around the room.

"This is still winter in Florida. You're crazy. The ocean is cold."

"I could warm you up when we come back. I feel like swimming in the nude in the pitch black and coming back here and making a fire. That is a fireplace and it does work, doesn't it?" She pointed across the room.

"I think we could work up a fire," he said, smiling.

"Come on…rip me out of my dress."

Chapter 12

When Mason and Whitefield met in the boardroom after lunch, Whitefield sat back in his chair, beaming.

"I don't know what's happened, but we've had a turn of good luck," Whitefield said. "The Arabs want the planes right away, and they will accept our supervisory pilots as delivery boys, and we ferry the jets to Paris. I've already given the okay to have flight plans filed for later this week. When the Arabs take possession, their New York bank will transfer the funds from their account to ours," Whitefield said.

"Great. We need a positive turn—although the sky could still fall. I'm not taking anything for granted these days."

"Nor am I, Hank, but it is better news than we have had in a long, long time."

"How is Trans-Globe doing on our routes north and west?"

"All right, but that temporary authority the CAB gave them so quickly will be snapped away the minute we get back into the airline business. What's the latest word on the strike?"

"They're talking today, if that means anything. I'll let you know. Has Ashley Channing contacted you yet?"

"Yes, she's already been in this morning. She's quite a beautiful woman…and intelligent. She seems to know exactly what she wants to do here, although I don't really like her approach, stealing an account like this." Whitefield tapped a pencil against the table. "I have a feeling she will stop at nothing to get this account. Is she after you, too?"

"She's after anybody who runs a company, who can throw an account her way."

"I have a strong feeling I've seen her before…" Whitefield said, rubbing a hand over his brow.

"She's been around in New York. Runs with the big boys. Lots of friends in important places."

"It was in New York, I'm sure of it, that I met her."

"She was a model in New York and her face has been on the cover of every major magazine in the country. She did some modeling in Paris, too."

"That could be it, but I think it was an airline meeting; yes, an industry cocktail party. Well, what does it matter?"

"She's never handled an airline account before. This is her first."

"Think she can do it?"

"Why not let her try? Our most recent campaign has helped start and prolong the strike with its exploiting of girls. Who knows, maybe she has something that will appease our women. White-field, get to know her. Take her out to dinner. I have a feeling we want her on our side now. She's a winner."

"I don't usually take advertising people out to dinner, Hank."

"Well, this time for me."

"She must really be after you."

"No, that's not it. I have a reason for asking you to extend our hospitality to her. It isn't personal. Just trust me."

"I don't know if my wife would understand my being out with such a creature as that," Whitefield said.

"Come on, Robert, you can explain that to your wife. Or don't bother. Just do it."

"You're the boss, Hank. All right, every courtesy to Ashley Channing."

"It won't be all that formal, Whitefield. She's an easy person to know."

They grinned at each other.

Mason was beginning to get hourly reports from his attorneys at the labor scene. The young lawyer who had rushed to his side to explain the action of one of the negotiators talked hurriedly and eagerly to Mason, relaying each incident at the bargaining table.

Issues and pieces of clauses that had been deadlocked throughout the strike were being settled, and the young attorney believed a contract would be in the mail in five more working days.

"Don't be too optimistic," Mason told him, trying to hold back his own exhilaration as the end of the nightmare became at least plausible. These events could not be chance, Mason thought. Ashley's influence was obviously working. No matter how she had achieved it.

Whitefield was right. She would stop at nothing to get Airways' account, although he did wonder at times why she needed it. Surely she had other accounts just as big. Why was she so fired up about his airline? He would not let his ego settle on the belief that she was after Hank Mason, and his airline only incidentally.

As Mason was dressing for dinner that night, he thought of Trina. Walking about his apartment, he felt a kind of springtime rushing through his veins. He was excited about seeing Trina, at the prospect of looking at her by candlelight, and his excitement continued to grow as he drove to her home.

The house where Trina's parents lived was set back in what he judged to be a couple of acres of wooded land off Indiantown Road in Jupiter. Tall Florida pine trees grew around the small, white frame house with green shutters covering the windows. Smoke from a red brick chimney puffed gray against the blue twilight. He liked this house and the yard and the rusty-coated Lab that licked at his pants leg as he made his way to the front door.

The woman who opened the screen door and led him into the living room was Trina's aunt, the woman told Mason. "Aunt Dorothy from North Carolina, a town you never heard of probably—Elk Park—western part of the state." She smiled at him from a cherubic face, her blue eyes reflecting a special warmth.

"Trina's mom and dad are out boating on the St. Lucie…that's the river just north of here," she said.

"You have quite a niece," he told Aunt Dorothy as he stood in front of the fireplace, his hands outstretched to catch the heat.

"From what I hear, you're quite an airline president, and I certainly do feel for you fellows that run businesses. My husband just ran a corner grocery, but the risks and headaches...employees never seem to see your side of the fence."

"Seldom," he said, admiring the small woman who seemed charged with energy and common sense.

Mason knelt down to stoke the fire and when he stood again, Trina was at his side. Her face was pink and flushed in the fire's light, and she smelled of lilacs and wild flowers, the kind he remembered picking in his boyhood.

"You're right on time," she said. There was an aura of sweetness and gentleness about her, and Mason felt the newborn urges of adolescence as he stood next to Trina in the small, comfortable room.

"We'll see you later, Aunt Dorothy," Trina said, kissing her aunt on the cheek.

"I'm glad I met you, Aunt Dorothy," Mason told the woman as she held the screen door for the couple. She waved to them as they drove away in Mason's MGB.

"You look beautiful, Trina," he said, glancing at her as he drove down the dirt ruts that led to the blacktop.

"Just in the dark," she smiled at him.

He felt a sudden surge of energy and vitality. No, he could not remember feeling so alive in years.

Heading north on U.S. 1, they talked about the mushrooming growth of the population on all the land that was left of the Gold Coast of Florida. When they stopped, they found themselves in Vero Beach, and Mason found an old, rustic seafood restaurant on the beach where they sat at a window table and watched the sea splash against the lighted rocks below.

After a lingering but comfortable silence between them, Mason felt Trina's eyes meet his. "I suppose we are like the waves out there.

We are born; we rise to a crest, break, and roll ashore. It is all too brief. Too terribly brief," she said.

"It doesn't seem brief sometimes…when there's trouble."

"No, I think you're right. When there's pain or sorrow, life seems endless," she said.

Leaning closer to her from across the table, he held out his hand and clasped hers in it. Her hand was warm and delicate, soft in his. "What do you want to do now with your life?"

"I don't know. Oh, there was a time when I was sure what I wanted to do. But this accident, this involvement in the strike, have made me see myself and other people in a different light…I actually wanted to work my way up in the Airways ranks or in the union. Be a stewardess supervisor or whatever else I could. I love flying. I still do—and the airline business. But I'm not sure it loves me."

"Sometimes I'm not sure of the same thing, but this has been my life since I was a boy. All I ever dreamed of was owning an airline and flying into the wild blue yonder. Funny, how we never really grow up from playing pilot or stewardess, or doctor or nurse."

"No, we don't. We are children…always."

"You know any job in the airline can be yours."

"You don't owe me anything, Hank."

"It's not that. I didn't say that because I feel I owe you a job. You're a talented, brave young woman, and I think you could have any future you choose."

"Here we are talking about business after all. And you're bothered by it all day and probably most nights."

"You're right. So, what have you been doing with yourself?"

"Reading, resting, thinking, getting a perspective."

"And what about this Doctor Jensen? You said he's helped you?"

"I had some bad moments in the hospital, nightmares that wouldn't stop. We became friends, and he showed me that life really wasn't closing in on me the way I thought it was. I've been seeing him off and on…." She stopped and looked away, pulling her hand from Mason's.

He felt a pang of jealousy rising in himself. "You must like him. Is there anyone else you see?"

"You know I have friends, Hank. I see them."

"Trina," Mason said, twisting in his chair. He was nervous suddenly, "If I asked you to be special to me…my life with women has not been the model of success. The truth is I haven't had a real relationship with a woman like you." He fingered a glass of water, hoping that she would interrupt him. He waited.

"I don't lead people on, you know," she said.

"I know." He wanted to kiss her and hold her at that moment, but he knew he could not spring his emotions on her now. Sitting back in his chair, he paused reluctantly. He had not ever restrained himself this way, but now, with this woman, he had to.

Not since high school days had he left a girl at her front door without at least a slight kiss, but he did Trina. She did not invite him in but simply disappeared with a wave of her hand behind the screen door.

As he drove back to Palm Beach, he realized she was not playing an intentional game of enticement with him. At this minute she could have gifts, a luxury apartment, a car, all the trappings that most glamorous young things longed for if only temporarily—but she was not buying that package. Trina Bellam was an unusual woman in these times, he decided. It was not so much the fact that he could not have her easily that intrigued him, he decided. Trina represented convictions and strength and caring. And if he wanted her, he would have to appeal to these qualities. He would have to offer her a wholeness. Was he willing to do that for any woman? He tried once with Lenoir, but Trina was not Lenoir.

The head of the law firm that held Lenoir's will was on Mason's private line at nine the next morning.

"Look," Porter Lamaretta said, and Mason could feel the lawyer leaning back in his chair, gnawing a fat cigar, "why not borrow a couple, three million against your wife's estate?"

"This could be considered an unethical, illegal discussion, Porter," Mason said.

"I'm your friend, Hank. This is just a friendly talk."

"I hear what you're telling me."

"You're still in a bind, Hank. This strike could go on indefinitely, and you have bills to pay. Now, I can arrange a private loan, unsecured at this point, just your signature. You're a good risk," Lamaretta laughed.

"I can't borrow against what I don't have, and besides, what is your fee and interest on such a loan?"

"My fee—a point or two, percentage I mean, of the total amount. And the interest, well, a few points above prime. You can't go wrong, Hank. This is ready cash. I know about the deal with the Arabs. That may not be, you know. These characters are just as slippery as we are…"

Mason wanted to strangle the obese attorney. How dare he dangle his dead wife's money over him. Mason yelled into the phone, "Porter, you're the lowest…"

"Think about it," Porter said.

Mason called Whitefield, and in the next few minutes he was looking at his executive vice president across his table. "You still think somebody is interested in buying this real estate we're sitting on?" Mason asked.

"What's wrong, Hank?"

"How sure are we of the Arab deal?"

"It's got snags now, but then all deals have those. Why?"

"We need money soon, and the real estate might be the answer in case the Arab thing falls through."

"Yes, it might be." Whitefield sat down. "But remember real estate is depressed right now, and I'm not sure we could get that kind of sale-leaseback we once talked about."

"We don't need this damn real estate anyway, and selling it is a way of getting the cash we need. How long would it take to put a deal together?"

"Well, it could take months. We don't have a ready buyer, Hank. You know how long it takes to get a commitment."

"How much could we raise?"

"Perhaps $30 million. It depends on the buyer. Perhaps more."

"And that would keep us comfortably afloat."

"At one time, some of the board insisted we were wrong to keep this much of our assets tied up in real estate. We shouldn't have trouble getting board approval."

"Get started on it. It's top priority."

"Have you heard anything on the strike?"

"Talks have broken down again. There's another power play. A third major union is trying to break this present leadership, and in general we have more of a mess. I may go to the officials of all the other unions under our roof."

"What about the plan with the Senator?"

"I don't know if that's for real or not. I can't trust it anyway, not now. Thinking back, I heard one side of that conversation Ashley had with her senator, and Ashley is in advertising. She can sell anything."

Whitefield rose from his chair, took off his glasses, and looked at Mason. "She is still a remarkable woman, Hank. She might have both of us believing we can conquer the world before all this is over."

"She might," Hank said, smiling. He wondered about Whitefield. Had he discovered Ashley, too?

It was the kind of day when he felt like making things happen. Mason wanted to call the most expensive condominium complex in South Florida and buy something huge and luxurious for Trina, but he knew he could not afford it now—and he realized she would not accept it if he handed her the deed and keys with no strings. Strange, he said to himself. They did not set another date, and yet he sensed she wanted to see him again...or were his signals all wrong? Did she feel sorry for him because his airline was in trouble and his wife had died?

He reached for the phone to call Trina. No, not so soon. Let her breathe.

"Miss Channing to see you," his secretary told Mason on the intercom.

"I came as soon as I heard. That damn horror of a strike. Fools. They're just fools. It isn't my friend's fault. There isn't anything he can do at the moment," Ashley spoke hurriedly. She was wide-eyed with anger.

"I never expected miracles from the senator or you. Take it easy. Sit down." Mason watched an unnerved Ashley Channing. She was animated, her hands flying as she talked.

"I did promise, and now it looks as if this is a deliberate botch by the union because they want retaliation against interference."

"There are some problems within the union, with two more unions trying to move in and take over. Things like that happen frequently in unions. It's not a new story."

"It's a bad reflection on me and my contacts. It means I don't have a crack at your account until this thing is ended. A lot of people are wondering, too, how you're surviving without being a member of the Mutual Aid Pact. Maybe you should join."

"No, that isn't the answer. I couldn't now anyway, Ashley. I'm going to meet with our union heads and soon. I don't want to threaten them, but I do want to make it plain that our employee count will have to shrink if and when we go back to work."

"That is a threat."

"It's a reality. And that's one I'll release to the press."

"You don't want to antagonize the unions, any of them."

"Of course I don't. I believe in the necessity for some unions. I don't always believe in the people who run the unions. Their egos and greed get in the way of what's best for their members. The bosses continue to draw salaries, and damn good ones, while the members go hungry during these long strikes. Members don't rebel often enough and put their own leaders under the gun. They accept them as mama and papa doing what's best—they think.

That's what I object to. If my beliefs antagonize the unions, hell, I'll have to antagonize them.

"Airlines and other industries haven't spoken up enough against the abuses of some unions. Do you know how much cargo is stolen every year from airlines? But we've taken it. We don't want to upset the unions, and we're afraid of bad press and the organized criminal elements within unions. So we're silent, and the shippers and the customers lose billions of dollars every year. Well, that's just *one* horror story, and it's not my problem right now. I don't have any cargo to ship these days."

"I suppose I've been no help at all, Hank. Thanks for not being angry at me."

"I have nothing to be angry about. How is your tour of the airline going?"

"Fine. Mr. Whitefield is most cooperative, although he doesn't tell me too much about the day-to-day running of the airline. You see, I'm building the campaign around facts, not froth. I'm selling sizzle and the steak. Your airline is going to look like today and tomorrow. Women are going to be featured but not in their usual sexist roles."

"You know, we still haven't bought this campaign yet. You may be losing a bundle by this kind of speculation. Aren't your other accounts suffering?"

"What kind of business woman do you think I am? I have associates minding other parts of the store. Besides, I think I've made an ally during my stay at Airways, haven't I?"

"Yes, I guess Whitefield is becoming a good friend, isn't he?"

"Remember, a woman scorned…" she said, laughing.

"I never knowingly make women angry," he said, putting his hands in his pockets, looking at his airplanes. "Did I ever tell you I once ran an airline" he added, abruptly changing the subject.

"Ever think of giving it all up?"

"To do what? This is my whole life. Or has been."

"What about staring a new airline?"

"Not today. It's impossible with the government planning every step you take in this business. I could in South America…maybe, but…our government's design, it seems, is to reduce the number of airlines in existence today, consolidate and squeeze some of us out. There may not be an Airways in a few years. Remember the railroads?"

"You mean you might sell or merge?"

"It could happen."

"What about your son? Wouldn't he take over the airline?"

"No, he has no real interest."

"Where is he, by the way?"

"At his mother's house. He's just resting. Making plans about his life—he'll probably go to school."

"Are you disappointed?"

"We've never been close. I haven't been much of a father. And to try and make it up now—that would be a sham. Maybe someday when he's a man and I'm wiser…I don't know. I feel a certain guilt. Let's not get into this."

"I have an idea. Let me cook dinner for you tonight, and we'll invite your son, too."

"No, that's too much."

"No, I insist. Call him. I won't accept you without him. Please," Ashley said, "I owe you so much."

"You don't owe me anything." He looked at her a long time, but he was thinking of Trina and being with her later.

"I'll let you know, Ashley." Mason did not like the hollow sound of his reply, and he wondered for an instant if Ashley detected just why he'd reacted to her invitation in that way.

When Mason got back to The Breakers, he called Trina. Her mother said she was out for the evening. With Doctor Jensen, he assumed. Why did he think that he had any hold over Trina? She did not belong to Hank Mason, he reminded himself. He had made no commitment to her. What did he expect? Surely, she felt something for him. The look in her eyes the night before…or was he imagining what he wished for?

Disappointed, he phoned Ashley and accepted her invitation. It occurred to him he should feel somewhat guilty. He was treating her like a runner-up. He shrugged it off. There was nothing second-best about Ashley—she was just different from Trina.

By the time he reached Ashley's home, his mood had totally changed. The house that Ashley Channing leased on the north end of the island was set behind tall ficus hedges. It looked like a mountain chalet with its weathered wood and expanses of windows. When Hank entered, he found Ashley and his son hovering over a brick barbecue pit in the corner of the sunken living room.

"We're trying to get this thing to work," Ashley said to Hank as she turned in his direction. "Bet you can do it in a second."

Just then, Everett got the match to spark the coals. A flame lurched up from the iron rack of the pit, through the red metal flue rising beyond the beamed ceiling, and up through the roof.

"I'm glad we could get together like this, Everett," Hank said.

"So am I," the boy said, poking the coals with long brass tongs.

"This isn't going to be a formal dinner, but I guarantee it's going to be good," Ashley said, busying herself with the candles and flowers at the table.

Watching them, Mason thought that it was pleasant to be in this setting—a woman getting dinner, his son helping. Everett and Ashley talked about the house, which he said he liked. She said she had taken it for a year with an option to buy.

"I want to learn to skin dive," Ashley said after dinner. "Could you teach me?" She looked at Everett.

"Sure, I'll have some time before I take my med school exams," Everett said.

"Then you have decided," Hank said, surprised at the casualness of his son's announcement.

"Yes, I have," the boy said.

Mason found himself at the barbecue pit, his eyes on the

smoldering coals. "It's really your choice," Hank said, facing away from him, and he was not sure Everett heard him or wanted to. It was his life, Mason thought, and it will always be hard for me to admit he's an adult. But why should I think I can turn him on like a robot? He looked at his son. "It's a wise decision, Everett. Ashley, thanks for an enjoyable… I appreciate it. I have some work to do."

"Do you really have to go?" She followed Mason to the door.

"Yes, I do. See you in the next few days." Mason paused, glancing back at Everett who seemed to be standing his ground. "Good night, Everett."

"Sure," the boy answered, heading in the direction of the kitchen.

"You're almost like strangers with each other," she said as they stood at the door. "Are you coming back here? I could wait up. Anyway, I'll be awake…" she said, her head leaning against the door.

He smiled but didn't reply.

As he drove south along the beach, a cold breeze rose off the sea, chilling his face. The air smelled fresh and salty and the night stimulated him. He longed to be with someone, to make love, to lie suspended in time away from his problems. No, not the right answers. He recognized that for the first time since Lenoir's death, he was beginning to feel in real possession of his thoughts and actions. He had been wandering around in a daze for years, and his awakening was building in him a whole new well of life.

Driving faster and heading for his office, he planned to clear his desk of the usual paper mill and call Whitefield. It was midnight, but Mason had lost regard for time when he entered the office and dialed Robert Whitefield. "I want a meeting this week, Whitefield, of all union heads. Any word on the deal for the sale of our real estate?" Mason could hear Whitefield breathing deeply.

"Yes, a buyer will take the deal. But the price is closer to 20 to 25 million, quite a cut from the 30 or 40 I envisioned. And, Hank, the Arabs will buy our planes, but this tabling of our decision means they will have time for more conditions."

"Bastards."

"You know the story of beggars."

"I didn't say I wouldn't take the real estate deal or renege on the plane sale either. I said they're both holding us up."

"The real estate terms are these. We get the cash.

"We lease it for 20 years and at the end of the term we have a buy-back privilege. What are you doing up at this hour of the night...or morning?"

"I felt like working. That's all. Go back to sleep or whatever you were doing."

Chapter 13

"Whitefield," Mason said, pacing back and forth in Whitefield's office the next morning at nine. "I'm tired of assing around. What time is that meeting you arranged with the unions?"

"Ten tomorrow morning, here in the boardroom. Washington was not the best site, with the talks moved there again, and so on. This union meeting is way off base. Nobody operates like this. The leaders are confused…"

"I don't want anybody else here. Not PR, no lawyers. Just you and me and the union leaders. We're coming out of that room with a definite course of action. We just can't go on any longer."

"This is crazy, crazy…"

Mason slammed his fist down on the chair in front of him. "I've taken the hopeful approach all along and it hasn't worked. I allowed Ashley to get involved. That was a mistake. So I'm crazy."

"*If* she did in fact get her Senator involved, he may have told her he would put a strong arm in just to make her happy and then did nothing."

"Yes, but I think he did say something to the union people in Washington, and that was all wrong. After this meeting tomorrow, we settle or the whole airline may be looking for jobs." Mason was quiet for a while. "And the deal with the Arabs is off. I'm not going to get rid of planes in the fleet unless it's our 747. One is too hard to maintain. If they want it, fine. If not—screw 'em."

"What new femme fatale has come over you?"

"It's been Ashley for the last month or so, Whitefield. You know that. But that's…I've got to get back to living again. The way I once did…"

"Yes," Whitefield took off his glasses and stared at his boss. Mason raced through the office door.

✈

Before the meeting with the union officials began, Mason sat alone in the boardroom. Here, he thought, he would be laying his position on the line. It was the kind of action he had never taken before, but he had to have a showdown. He could not stay adrift any longer. He should have done this a long time ago, but now he had only the future to think about.

Two representatives from each of the seven unions with contracts at Airways filed into the boardroom and took seats around the oval table.

Mason sat at one end of the table and facing him was the lone woman in the room, the top leader now of the flight attendants' union. He looked at her a moment and thought that Trina might have been here today had it not been for the so-called accident.

Noise was blanketed out of the room—except for the turning of platform chairs and an occasional clank of a pencil against the table. A few of the men lighted cigarettes, one tore at the tip of his cigar. There was nod of a head here and there from men Mason had met over the years, but no one was especially outgoing. The woman looked in Mason's direction but quickly changed her focus to a yellow legal pad.

"This isn't going to be a formal meeting," Mason said. "I'm glad you're all here, that you agreed to meet with me. You probably know the status of the union negotiations from the morning papers. They're stalled—we aren't getting anywhere. I called this meeting to tell you about a decision I have made for the good of the company and the good of many of the employees—before the gossip mill gets the whole story out of proportion.

"I'm entering into merger talks this week. This is not a threatening act. It's just a fact of life. We cannot go on like this without income and see our stock tumble and our equipment lost. I have had merger offers, quite a number of them. So…"

The union people looked at one another. Worry showed in all their faces, Mason thought.

One man, from the mechanics' union, raised his hand.

"Mr. Mason, this is a threat to us all. Our jobs are at stake here. The surviving airline, and I don't think from what you said it will be Airways, will have to have layoffs. That's us. You're forcing us into a labor crisis. This is against all labor relations."

"I can't help that," Mason said, rising and sliding his hands in his pockets. "I only know what has to be done for the survival of this company, to keep it alive so that it's worth something to another airline, where some of your jobs will remain."

The woman spoke up next. "This is the worst kind of threat to settle the strike. You're backing my union into a corner. This is…" The girl's pale face flushed red. She was pretty, Mason thought, but no Trina. After her remarks, she sat rigid against the back of her chair. She bowed her lips and tapped the point of her pencil on the pad.

One of the others interrupted her. "Look, my people, the communications workers, are ready to cross the picket lines. This has been the longest strike in the airline's history and if we go on this way, most of us won't have jobs to go back to." He glared at the girl. "I think Mr. Mason is trying to save the company, and in his shoes I might say the same damn thing."

The woman burst in, leaning forward. "You're trying to settle our strike in this room, and that's illegal and our union can take Mr. Mason and his airline to federal court for this. We're all risking lawsuits by our members for even being here."

Mason stood again. "Just a moment. We need some order. I did not call us together to argue or debate. I have made my point."

"But we haven't made ours," the woman shouted, springing to her feet. "You want to wage war amongst us."

"I want no such thing," Mason said. "These are the facts. If I have backed you into a corner as a result, then that's that. I have an airline with huge capital investments and thousands of employees to protect. Some of those employees are your members who might have jobs in a merged airline but won't have in a bankrupt one. If there are any questions, I'll answer them." Mason tried to control the rage thrashing through him. Getting mad was not the answer.

Retaliating now, before the people who could turn the tides for him, would destroy his plans.

The mechanics' union head rose. "I'm speaking for myself and my union now, and I don't want to get anybody's nose out of joint when I say this. I think we've all had enough of this strike, and I don't think anybody wants to cross the line or else we'd have it done to us right back. And that breaks down the whole labor system. I do think my union is going to ask the flight attendants to do everything to end this thing right away. The flight attendants would do the same for us. Now, I've been through a merger and a lot of jobs are preserved. Mine wasn't, though, because I was a young mechanic with no seniority. But a bankrupt airline, nobody's got work. So, ma'am, I would urge you to go back to your union and you, too, sir," he nodded in the direction of the male flight attendant, "and tell your people that you're getting with it and now. That you all are going to settle."

"Hear, hear," shouted one man and there were loud approvals around the table.

Mason watched the woman. She was about to explode as she whispered to the other representatives from her union.

"I thank you all for coming, and I pray we see an end to this for all of us," Mason said. There was no need to press issues. These men—and woman—knew his strategy.

Every member of the group shook hands with Mason at the end of the meeting—except the flight attendants' leaders. When the woman met Mason at the door of the boardroom, she stopped short. "Go screw yourself for a change," she said.

Only Whitefield was close enough to Mason to catch the remark, and he shook his head at Mason.

"You get immune," Mason said.

Mason closed the door behind him and went back to the boardroom table, where he sat alone to collect himself. He had done it now. There might be physical violence among the union members, his stock could take a plunge, the board members could fire him as president and there could be a merger. But then the strike could end, too. Mason went to Whitefield's office.

"My, you've done it. Talk's all over the industry we're merging. I've had five calls in the last 15 minutes. Are we merging as you said? Incidentally, you handled yourself fine in that meeting even if we'll be sued for 100 reasons."

"Thanks. Yes, we are doing something, legal, illegal."

"Have you entered into an agreement in principle with somebody?"

"Hell, you know I haven't."

"But you're going to? You want me to set up the talks?"

"No," Mason said. "I have everything under control. I do want you to get a letter of intent from the buyer on this land. I need a deed now."

"Okay, that's at the head of my list." Whitefield paused and looked at Mason. "Is this the rabbit in the hat? Do you really intend to go through with the merger talks? A buyer could sue if you used merger talks as a bribe, entered into talks in bad faith."

"I know, I know. Don't worry about it. Round up the board up for me. I'll need their votes on this land sale. You can do the explaining. And the Arabs…"

"Yes, Hank…I know about them. I got a report this morning from the FBI out of New Orleans. They think now it may have been a band of anti-Arabs that bombed the 747. One of them has cracked. He may be for real. He may not."

"The solution doesn't bring our people back, or our plane."

"No." Whitfield was thoughtful. "The insurance questions may drag on for months. We have no clause that applies to bombings or acts of violence."

Mason nodded thoughtfully, then left. Once back in his office, he phoned Trina. She was not at home. Again. That made him angry. "I have to see her this evening, Mrs. Bellam," he told her mother. "I'll be up about eight."

✈

That night, Mason was at Trina's front door when he said he would be. Trina looked at him through the screen. She wore no makeup and was dressed in faded blue jeans and a green pullover sweater. "Come in," she said. "Sit down," she told him as they walked into the living room.

Taking a seat on the sofa, he watched her as she stood near the fireplace. There was the faint crackle of the burning logs and the lonely songs of wild birds in the woods around the house. "I've wondered how you were. I've called..."

"Yes, I know. It's just that...I had nothing to say to you," she said.

"You could have told me that."

"I suppose. But I'm not ready..."

"For what? What do you think I had to say to you?"

"I don't know. I'm confused."

"I haven't said anything to confuse you, have I?"

"Yes, yes, you have." She folded her arms, turning away from him.

He stood, still looking at Trina and then moved toward her. His passions told him to take her in his arms and comfort her, but his good sense held him back. "This feeling between us, Trina, is more than casual or else I would have tried to have you a long time ago. You have thought about us, then?"

"Of course I have. The other night..."

"What about the other night?"

"Nothing, I don't want to get into any discussions. I just can't."

Mason was baffled. She was encouraging him, he thought, and at the same time was pushing him away. Well, he had never been rebuffed in his life...this way.

He was quiet for a moment. "You may not believe this, Trina, but I have not really cared for any woman in a long time...since my wife, the first years of our marriage. I began to work and love my business more than I did my wife and child, and I fell into my own trap. It was easy to satisfy my body with beautiful women and booze. I was exhausted half the time, and I didn't think about love or loving. But now, now I think about the possibility of love."

Tears came to Trina's eyes, and she moved slowly back and forth in the room.

Why should she be crying now when he was saying words to her he had not uttered in decades? Some women did cry when they were happy. Were these tears of joy? "What is it? What's wrong, Trina?"

"You can't do anything about my problems, Hank. I'll have to solve them all by myself."

"I can listen. I can always listen. Come for a drive, a long drive with me up the coast."

They rode in his open MGB for miles without talking. It was the kind of calm that excited him and filled him with longing and simultaneously brought him a certain peace. Having not to speak, to force himself to bring up subjects he cared nothing for—this was a relationship that could endure. Being quiet, gliding through the night together—these were the subtleties of understanding. He had not experienced such a bridge with another human being since those first times with Lenoir. That had been so long ago.

When they returned to Trina's house, she did not ask him in but simply made her exit and walked to the front door as if she were not aware of his presence.

What had he done to her? There seemed to be no bond between them any longer. It was as if she had created a void, a down-under place where if he chose to stay, he would be miserable. Without saying good night, he got back in his car and drove away... mystified.

"Doctor Jensen is here," Mason's secretary told him over the phone.

"I have no appointment with the doctor...but send him in."

Doctor Jensen, a tall young man with dark hair and dark brown eyes, held out a lean hand to Mason.

"What's wrong with Trina?" Mason asked, startled by the doctor's visit.

"I guess my appearance here implies there is something wrong with her. It's very complex."

"How?" Mason said. He stood with his hands on his hips, eyeing the doctor's every feature.

"I wanted a few words with you."

"Sure, sit down," Mason said, taking a chair himself. "I don't quite understand."

"Trina and I have become friends, and I am concerned about her and her mental outlook."

"What are you trying to say?" Mason leaned against the back of his chair.

"I told you. Trina is my friend. A dear friend."

"And what do you want me to do?"

"The beating Trina took by the union or whomever, the physical beating was much more involved than she may have told you."

"What do you mean?"

"She was attacked sexually by men…and women that night."

"Oh, my God!" Mason's stomach churned.

"She was raped by a man and a woman and then…well, there were other brutalities. It's all sick, and she probably won't tell you about it for a long time."

"No, she never mentioned…I never suspected anything like this." Mason's face was crimson. He could not believe what the doctor had told him.

"I didn't think you knew and you should…" the doctor stopped. "You see, I know she cares about you. And that's really why I'm here. I care about her as much as she cares about you…I may as well admit that."

"What can I do to help her?" Mason was pensive, sick for Trina.

"Be patient. The wrong move, sexually, I mean, from you could destroy her. I'm not trying to tell you how to behave. I just don't want her hurt. Her behavior may be difficult to interpret from time to time. This was a devastating experience."

"Yes, yes, of course."

"A man of your reputation could be dangerous for Trina, especially now."

"What right have you...you think I'm just using her?"

"I can't judge that, Mr. Mason. I hope you're not." The doctor folded his arms and crossed his legs.

Pompous ass, Mason thought. He wanted to draw up the young buck who sat before him and punch him in the face. He wanted to see his blood stream across the room, but what would that accomplish? This man had come to help Trina, Mason knew. "You must be in love with her to come here and say these things to me." Mason wanted a response. "I'm glad to know all this, Doctor Jensen. She might be damaged mentally for a long while then?"

"She might be," the doctor said. He walked toward the door of Mason's office. "That's all I have to say except I'll offer her all the medical help she needs. Only you can really help her beyond the medicine. She thinks she can solve this herself. You could convince her to get all the professional care she needs."

"Yes," Mason said. He followed the doctor to the threshold of his office and offered his hand. "I don't expect that we'll be great friends, but I do respect you for coming here. I won't forget it. I'll do everything I can for Trina."

"I hope so."

Mason shivered when he recalled the night that Trina was attacked. So that was it. The experience of savage beating and rape. He would have to talk to the police again and to Trina. He had to force the authorities and the courts to punish the animals who hurt Trina. They would strike at somebody else when they felt like it. Just as he reached for the phone, Ashley walked into his office.

Dressed in violet, she seemed a mist and to float into the room. Mason liked the floral cologne she wore. For a minute she took his mind off his problems. "How would you like to have lunch with me?" she asked.

"No," he said, shuffling papers on his table. She came close to him, and when he stood up she brushed her hand against his face.

"Come on, I have something to ask you."

At Petite Marmite on Worth Avenue, they had taken a corner table amid hanging ferns and tall potted palms. Just as they finished lunch, they were spotted by a photographer. Ashley offered the short, balding man with glasses a toothy smile, and Mason looked at him blankly.

"You could have grinned for the man," Ashley said.

"I hope they won't use that anywhere."

"Well, I hope they do. I think he takes pictures that are used in the *Palm Beach Daily News*. It's not a bad little paper to appear in. Everybody who's anybody tries to make it in that little sheet...one time or another."

"I don't recall being anybody."

"You are, you are. You can't fight that, Mr. Mason. Say, your son and I have become good friends over the last few days. We've done some skin diving and had dinner. I think he likes me. And I think he's special."

"What's your angle with him?"

"To get through to his father and make friends of the father and son."

"I don't think anybody can do that."

"I can," she said, sipping her Manhattan.

Mason studied her face for a minute: the flawless skin, the wide, pink glossy lips, the shining hair, her impeccable dress. How could she repair the damage between a man and his child, a void that had been nourished all the child's life. Mason was only a boy himself when he became a father. "How do you propose to do this, Ashley?"

"I thought you'd never ask. Your son has never known a family life and it's about time he did. It's not too late now, you know."

"You want to marry him and have a family?"

She laughed. "No, but you're close. I want to marry you."

Mason leaned forward and whispered to her. "I think you're wild."

She laughed again and he did, too. "I'm serious, all right. You're free, handsome, accomplished. I think we make a great team. And your son does, too."

"You've talked to him about this then?" Mason lighted a cigarette.

"Yes."

"You don't waste any time, do you?"

"I can't afford to. Time is all I have, and a degree of talent. Well, what do you say?"

"I've never been proposed to. I'll have to think it over."

"You're not taking this to heart, are you? I want to be married to you. I mean that." Her smile disappeared.

Mason looked at her for a long time, trying to decide if she was brilliant or crazy. Maybe there was that fine line.

"I want a family. We'd have one with your child, and I'd like our own. A baby of our own."

"My God, Ashley. You want marriage and a child. When did you decide that? Aren't you going overboard trying to win my account?"

"I've wanted children for a long time. I just never realized it before. This had nothing to do with business."

"I never said I was serious, Ashley, and I certainly never thought of another family."

"You ought to. You're still young, and what have you got to look forward to, really?"

"Wait a minute, Ashley."

"All the elements are right for us. I know we could be a family, Hank. How much do you want your son—and another chance to raise a child?"

Mason hesitated and looked down at his empty Scotch glass. "With all my being, I want my son to be a son, but that's all over now. You can't roll back the years and start over. He isn't a baby. Our life patterns are all molded."

"You're talking as if you were both 90 years old. He's still flexible and open to change, at least. Who knows, he might be president of Airways one day."

"Look, Ashley, I don't want to play around with these kinds of emotions. It's too painful."

"All right, I know when to quit—for now. But think of it. A family right at your fingertips. We could have everything. Real happiness. I may not hold the offer open forever."

"I can't let boys and women make decisions for me, Ashley."

"What does that mean?" she asked, tightening her lips and raising her eyebrows.

"You know what that means. I think we ought to get out of here now."

"And where do we go? To your bed or mine?" she set her coffee cup down, bracing it while she waited for a reply.

"I have to get back to work, and so do you, if you want my account."

"Then you mean I do have it. How close is the strike to being ended? I can call my Senator…"

"You do that and you'll never see anybody again. I've set things in motion, I think, and we may be seeing a settlement soon."

Ashley dropped Hank off at his office, where again he tried to make the phone call he had in mind before lunch. This time Whitefield interrupted him.

"I think the strike is going to be over sooner than you and I thought this time," Whitefield said.

"What's the latest report?"

"Washington just called. The union reps from here have descended on the capital and are still sitting out in the halls waiting for negotiators to break for lunch. When that comes, you know what will happen. They'll apply personalized pressure."

"That's what I was planning on."

Whitefield laughed and sat down. "Hank, your bluff worked. The merger, that did it. You do know these union people, and, well, all of us. We're all deathly afraid of mergers."

"I'm not sure it was a bluff." Mason put his head back against his chair.

"Don't talk like that, Hank. It's dangerous. You may convince yourself you want to sell. You could not live without this airline. It's the one thing that sustains your life."

"I've got to find something else. Look how close I've come to losing everything. I'm still close. Right at the edge."

"No, you're far away. The rumors are that you will be a very rich man upon the reading of your wife's will."

"It's ironic, isn't it? Most of the people who know me and know of me think I am rich. And how much could I raise right now in cash without selling my stock in Airways? How long could I live?"

"You're still rich by most standards."

"You have more in cash than I do, by far, Whitefield. I've worked like a dog most of my life and this is what I have to show for it—it's all right here. I can't count my wife's money. I hardly worked for that. My son will be rich. He should have everything that belonged to Lenoir. And being rich is not what my life is all about. It never has been."

Mason's private line rang. "Yes," he said, cupping the phone, telling Whitefield it was Washington. "They have agreed verbally. I see. Well, hell yes, I'm relieved. But we will have to wait until that damn contract is ratified by members until we rejoice. Give my thanks to our entire team up there, and I'll be in touch with them later. Fine." He returned the receiver to its cradle, then took a deep, slow breath.

Mason turned to Whitefield. "That's it. Those union people who listened to me here have done it. The flight attendants' leaders have approved a contract, a reasonable one: a standard-of-living escalation clause that I expected, uniform approval involving the company and the members, retirement and dental care insurance provided by the company. Well, that's about it. I was a bastard about all these items at first, except for the salary increase. We got what we wanted. We can live with it over the next three years of the contract, but then the contract has to be ratified, and I will not count my eggs this time until they are in that basket. A lot could happen. Violence. We've seen it before. So, let's hope and wait."

Chapter 14

Mason's secretary said she did not know the voice on the line, and the caller would not identify himself. She told Mason the man said it was urgent and that was all.

"Okay," Mason said. "I'll take it." He pressed the lighted button down on his phone base. Crank call, he thought.

"Look, Mr. Mason, big man. Your little chick, the one up in Jupiter, is gonna be carved into shavings if there's any more buttin' in on union business. See? Understand? *Comprende?*"

The voice was a young male's, Mason thought. Mason did not answer but buzzed his secretary and told her to get the airline's switchboard to trace the call. "Yeah, go on. Tell me more," Mason said.

"Another thing, we don't like to be scared to death about losing our jobs. Merger fever. A lot of us are gettin' it. So, no more of that either. Or that little dish will be all down the drain." There was a click.

Mason knew the operator did not have time to track down the caller's location. He slammed the phone down. He had to alert the police and Trina and get her away from there.

In the next few minutes, Mason told the chief of airport detectives about the call, and he was assured Trina Bellam would have 24-hour protection at her home in Jupiter. Mason should never have dismissed the guards he assigned Trina when she left the hospital, but she had insisted.

Moments after arranging the guards, Hank was in his car and speeding toward U.S. 1 to Jupiter. He found Trina at home.

"I don't want to alarm you, Trina, but I've had a threat from a union person or sympathizer. Or maybe he's just a nut of some kind who's been following our crisis in the newspaper or on TV. But I can't take any chances. You have to listen to such rot these days with all the sick bastards running around loose. I want you away from this state, maybe even this country."

"But I can't just leave. Where would I go and how do I know I'd be safe anywhere?" she said.

"It may be nonsense, the threats about you, but we can't risk it."

Trina reached for a copy of the newspaper that carried candid shots of Mason and Ashley in a column of celebrity news.

Mason's face flushed red. "She's working on an ad campaign, but that's hardly important now."

Trina stared at him. There was a bitterness in her face. "You have a stash of girls everywhere, don't you?"

"You don't believe I do that now, do you?"

She looked away from him, her hands beginning to shake. Then she studied his face.

"Trina, I've got to help you after what you've been through, the hell, the absolute hell you've been through because of me. I can't take any chances with your life. I am responsible."

"What do you know about it?"

"I know everything that's happened, Trina." His voice dropped, the frenzy gone from his manner. "It's awful, but we can overcome bad times and forget…"

"Jensen told you, didn't he? I begged him not to tell anyone."

"It isn't important how I found out, Trina. It's only important that nothing more happens to you. I won't let it."

"I'm safe. I have my family."

"You also have 24-hour police protection from now on, and I'm hiring a private agency of my own, in spite of what you may say."

"But why? Why does anybody want to hurt me now?"

"They want to hurt me through you, Trina. And they can be brutal…as you've found out."

There was a quiet between them. He stood beside the sofa where she sat. "We're in this together, Trina, whether we like it or not. I'm sorry to be dragging you along, but we've got to fight it out."

"I suppose we are."

Her voice was vague but he could not blame her. If only he could turn back time. He would never have gotten her involved, but then he never would have discovered her either.

"I feel as though I'm suffocating sometimes," she said. "It's more than this latest episode. I've felt this way a long time."

It was the wrong time to tell her now…how he felt. She was trapped in memories of horror, and he had to be patient. If only he could be.

"I have to sort out my life," she resumed, "and the nature of human beings. I've had trouble doing that. You just can't ask me to go away somewhere. Alone. My parents would be lost. I'd never stop running, you know. And I refuse to run from labor unions or insane people or whoever is out there."

"I just want the best for you, Trina."

"Go back to work, Hank, and don't worry about me anymore."

Hank desperately wanted to take her in his arms, to hold her, console her—but he knew he could not…not yet. Her request for him to leave, and to leave her alone, was proof enough. But he was loath to leave her like that, despite the tension in the room. Only after Mason spotted a squad car in front of the Bellam house did he decide to head back to the office. "They're here watching over you already. They'll give you instructions. And you must follow their advice," Mason said. He kissed her on the cheek and left.

Whitefield flew into Mason's office, papers askew in both hands. His face and bald head were sweaty and red.

"What the hell is wrong with you? You've never been this flustered in your life!" Mason stood back and looked at his colleague and then helped him unload his papers onto the table.

"Many, many things have happened since news of the strike settlement hit the newsstands. I have a letter of commitment on the real estate deal, a firm offer on the 747 at $20 million, all cash and delivery in 30 days—all of this topped off by a lawsuit from our present ad agency if you don't stop flaunting your relationship with Ashley Channing. Breach of contract, I believe our attorneys called it."

"I think we might get more than that for the 747 with the spare parts thrown in. You can renegotiate. I'm glad about the real estate deal. And it's nobody's business about me and Ashley."

"You sound like your old rotten self."

"You sound like somebody I don't even know. You're coming unglued."

"Well," Whitefield rubbed his head, "I have a lot on my mind." He followed Mason's every move.

"We all do, Whitefield. What in particular, though, is it with you?"

"I may as well be honest with you. Another airline has approached me for a top spot, Hank. I suppose that's at the basis of my condition."

"Don't tell me that's never happened to you before. You're damn great and everybody knows it. Mainly me."

"An offer of this kind with this kind of money, Hank, has never been made to me. They've mentioned a long-term contract."

"Do you want to take it, Whitefield?"

"You know how I feel about Airways, and you, Hank." He breathed heavily.

"If you want out, I won't hold you. Although I need you like I've never needed you, now and in the months around the corner. You've got to know that. This is the worst time…but I still won't stop you."

"We won't talk about this again unless I decide to leave, Hank."

"All right, Whitefield. That's that then."

"Now, what's happening with you?"

"I got a call. A crank call, I thought at first. It was from a union employee or somebody who's off his nut and has somehow involved himself in our situation. He knows a lot about me anyway. He's threatened Trina's life unless I lay hands off any more union interference and if there is any known merger business, well, that could cause fireworks for Trina. The police know all about it, and I have protection for Trina."

"This is an insane world we live in."

"I guess we just have to ride it out. I can't blame the union. That's an easy out. It could be anybody. A sick mind somewhere."

"Oh, we have lots of borderline cases right here at this airline and when people are up against the wall—no jobs, no money— anything like this can happen. You're a target, a scapegoat."

"Sometimes I do think I ought to give up this company."

"You'll never do it, Hank. Never." Whitefield turned to an envelope from which he took a commitment letter to purchase and lease back to Airways all of the airline's property surrounding the airport.

"I don't want to sign that yet," Mason said.

"Hank, do you realize how much negotiating this took? If you turn it down now and you want it again you can kiss the major lending community good-bye. I've shopped this pretty well and carefully."

"Table it a few days. That's all. I know what I'm doing."

"This is not a bad deal, Hank. As for the Arabs, the price for the 747 is realistic and fair, considering it's just one plane we have to sell."

"No, hold off on the plane sale, too."

"You're not depending on the end of the strike for all the answers, I hope."

"We'll see. We'll see. In the meantime, tell Ashley to get her ads ready to go. I like some of the things she's shown me. If that damn ad agency threatened to sue us, I don't want them around here anymore. Get rid of them. Just fire their asses right now. And I want their ads canceled."

"But they have commercials shot and print ads ready to go. They'll sue us."

"Just get them to send us a bill for everything. Talk to the attorneys to see exactly how our contract reads—I think they are harassing me because I'm seeing an advertising hotshot. You know, I never really liked their campaigns anyway. Slimy, most of it. I'm tired of their sex pitch, believe that or not. It's a bore. Besides, the union has some legitimate gripes about their most recent ads. Can 'em all. Tell Ashley to fire away."

"All right," Whitefield sighed. He collected his papers from the table.

When Mason's outside general counsel called from Washington minutes later, Mason sat on the edge of his chair.

"No," the attorney said, "It's not about the strike. That's coming along fine, I understand. No, this concerns something a lot bigger. Someone has approached me today, the president of Trans-Globe. You've never had any dealings with them, as I understand it. They want to buy Airways. It's that simple."

"You mean an attorney can state things that simply? Well, I never!" Mason laughed. "I can talk to the president but not here and not by phone at all. It would have to be in New York at the company suite. And I want no one at all to know about this besides the three of us. No one on your staff, not even your secretary. You make all the calls, et cetera. Make him understand it's for exploratory purposes only. I'll be in New York tomorrow all day. I have other business there."

Mason wondered why he had been so eager. Was he really trying to sell? He felt himself still acting out of panic, without direction. Well, what the hell did he have to lose by just talking about selling? The idea of leaving the agony of hanging by a shoestring every day tempted him. He pictured himself free of his hourly affairs with the telephone, his bouts with disaster or threat of it. He could pay all his debts, sell his stock, and retire. Retire to what?

Mason called Trina as soon as he arrived in New York.

"No, nothing has happened," she said. "Really, you ought to stop worrying about me. I've got two sets of protection and my parents. I'm fine."

"I'll be away for a few days and when I get back I want to talk something over with you."

"All right," she said. Her voice was calm, and Mason was relieved to find she was unharmed and steady.

When Ashley rang Mason a few minutes after he talked to Trina, he was alarmed. "How did you know I was here?" he asked Ashley.

"Relax, I just figured that's where you were. I'm coming up myself. I have business with my staff. I'm grateful, Hank, about getting the account. I still can't quite believe it."

"You have what you want, Ashley."

"Almost. I want to see you in New York. Will you have dinner with me tomorrow night?"

"I have appointments until late."

"With someone I know?"

"I don't think so."

"Why were you so concerned that I knew where you were?"

"I was just surprised. I wanted to be completely alone. I have business with my banks."

"Money trouble?"

"Why wouldn't I have them?"

"You're not thinking of selling your stock or anything like that?"

"That wouldn't help my airline's position or mine very much. Do you think I could sell at the current price? Besides I'm governed a bit by the Securities and Exchange Commission on such matters as selling."

"I don't know what the price is. I'll look. You do sound gloomy and down."

"I've sounded that way for quite a long time. In fact, probably all the time we've known each other, Ashley."

"Then I have to change that. We'll have dinner at my apartment whenever you finish those meetings."

"Fine," he said and wrote down her address on East 55th Street.

The next morning at nine, the president of Trans-Globe arrived at Mason's suite. Gabriel Bachrach was tall, slender, graying at the temples and looked to Mason like thousands of other well-heeled New York businessmen.

Mason was conscious for a moment that Bachrach did not understand the incongruities before him—Mason's worn, brown suede jacket, his sports shirt, his unpolished brown leather loafers, all served up with French antiques and Persian rugs in the elegant apartment. Then Bachrach seemed to brush aside the surroundings and opened what Mason recognized as a Gucci black leather attaché case. Bachrach was deliberate, organized, and determined, Mason observed.

"I know your airline well, Mr. Mason, and I like what I know. We would have no intention of seeing you leave what you have built."

"You just want to pull all the strings. Well, that's understandable. What else do you propose?"

"You know that new routes to Europe and the Middle East are just not going to be awarded by the CAB for a long time. And particularly to Airways, which will need to recover from a long strike and build its business back."

"You may be right, Bachrach."

"We have no doubt you can win back that business, but with Trans-Globe serving some of your routes as we are now, we will probably apply for permanent certification to compete with you."

"That will take money and time and we'd fight you every step of the way. The CAB often rules for the underdog and in this case— we are."

"All right, then, Mr. Mason, let us talk on more cooperative terms. We would want to keep you on in the United States as top vice president with your chosen staff. We would offer a three-for-one stock trade-off and a place for you on the board. You would name your salary and other benefits. The maintenance base would have to be worked out in this country. I think the employee shrinkage factor will be the most changed aspect of our total operation. And there's the matter of the unions—all of the trouble you've have with them.

"We have a great deal of power behind our airline, Mr. Mason, and we can eventually win the routes you have now if you don't sell to us or someone else. It's simpler for everybody to merge. Trans-Globe would be the largest airline in the world if Airways became part of us—outside of Aeroflot—in route miles and passengers flown."

"It's a big dream, Mr. Bachrach."

"I do not like the dream state, Mr. Mason. I like to make things happen. Apparently so do you. I have been studying airlines to buy for the past five years. The strike and your financial situation were not the only motivating factors behind my plan to see you and discuss merging with you. You have created an excellent airline in every respect. We would not be talking if we considered Airways to be in sad shape."

"I'll be back with you at the end of the week, Bachrach. I appreciate your interest and faith in my airline."

Mason shook hands with his visitor and showed him to the door and went back to the sofa. He felt empty and lonely. This was what many businessmen envisioned—building up a company, selling it, and sitting back to relax and let somebody else do all the worrying. But he couldn't let go that easily. He was too fired up with energy and plans for his airline to bow out. Still he did have the chance, and he needed to leave that door open now.

Chapter 15

Mason walked to Ashley's apartment house down Fifth Avenue. Her building was small and handsome with a fancy uniformed doorman, heavy oak furniture in the lobby, and a fancy elevator that took Mason to the seventh floor.

When Ashley met him at her door, she threw her arms around him. "Congratulations, darling," she said, kissing him. Her words melted on his tongue.

He pulled back, the scent of her perfume clouding his thoughts for a minute. "For what? Finding my way here?"

"No, silly. The union settlement, of course. Aren't you excited?" She waited. "No, I suppose you don't believe it. I've already lined up my staff for the work on the account, bought time on TV, finished newspaper ads for you to look at..."

"Holy crap. Let me use your phone."

She handed him a phone from a nearby table. He dialed Whitefield's number while his heart pounded.

"Where have you been, Hank? I've called everywhere for you," Whitefield shouted over the phone so that Ashley heard him.

"I'm in New York. Hell, let's skip that now. It is true—the strike is over."

"Yes, yes, it is. The contract has been ratified. There have been some local fights, some bloodletting, so to speak. A mechanic was shot in our parking lot. I don't know why he was here. He's in stable condition now, though. There have been some bomb threats. The main thing is the contract approval. We crank up in two days. Are you coming back here?"

"Of course. You know I am. And Whitefield, thanks for taking care of everything. I had important business here."

"Meanwhile, what do I tell our lenders? You know this is really bad business to back out like this..."

"Under these circumstances, we can call the shots. Tell them we're sorry. I'll follow up with visits and amends."

"There is something else. Porter Lamaretta called me when he couldn't reach you. There will be an early reading of Lenoir's will, and he wants to schedule it this week. You had better call him."

"Well, everything comes at once." Mason set the phone down on the table. "The contract is signed. The strike is over, and we have an airline to run again. I'm numb."

"This means your life can begin again…in a real way."

"Yes, it does." Mason rubbed his hand over his forehead. His eyes were tired but a sense of relief spread over his whole body. Somehow he felt like a walk in the rain. Hard to arrange that. He looked at Ashley, her hair loose, falling around her face like silk. She might have stepped from a vision, he thought, looking like this. She was womankind. Soft. Colorful. Desirable. She might have been Trina or Francine or any one of the beautiful women he had made love to. He wished he had clarity in this moment. He wished for Trina. He asked for a Scotch and drank it straight down. Then he moved toward the vision which became a warm, enchanting body.

Suddenly, he pulled away from Ashley.

"What's wrong?" she said.

"It isn't you, Ashley. It is not you." He could not go through with making love to her now. Despite her splendor and the joy of the moment, he simply could not indulge himself, lose himself the way he had before.

He went back to The Pierre, packed, and caught a cab for LaGuardia. A new life was ahead of him now. He had another chance to set things right, and he could not botch a single element.

When he got to the South Florida airport, his first stop was his own hangar where blue-white floodlights made daylight of the pre-dawn. There was the smell of jet fuel and cabin cleansers and fresh paint all around him.

Mason waved to the men he saw in their mechanics' uniforms, their white plastic hardhats casting off reflections in the bright work lights. There was a briskness in their steps. Their actions were contagious. He, too, was filled with a sense of purpose and direction, for, within hours now, his planes would be up there again, in the sky where they belonged. Thoughts of his talk with Bachrach in New York were hazy as he left the hangar and headed for his office.

Whitefield was already at work, Mason learned when he called him at home. Whitefield's wife told Mason he had spent the whole night at the airline—in his office or at the hangar.

"Get your ass in here," Mason told Whitefield. "We've got an airline to run. Where are you?" Mason threw his phone back down.

Within five minutes, Whitefield was sitting in front of Mason with several folders in his lap. "I just came from talking with the mechanics. I see you got the red-eye special from New York. I didn't know you'd make it this fast. Don't forget to check with Porter about the will. He called me twice at home last night. He's already contacted your son, and they want to get the will reading over with."

"I don't want to go through that business but I suppose I must—sometime."

"Our ads break tomorrow on TV and radio and in the papers. We've had excellent news coverage on the signing."

"First flight will be in New York, huh? Good. Well, we're in business again, and it's damn hard to believe. It seems we've been staring at each other in this graveyard for years. You decided about that job you've been offered?"

"I'll let you know if and when I do. Don't worry about it now." Whitefield headed for the door and then turned around. "I remember when I first saw Ashley—it was with the president of Trans-Globe, Bachrach. It was a security analysts meeting in New York. Not that this means anything really."

"It could mean a great deal, Robert. You're sure about that?"

"I'm sure."

"Who knows? Maybe she's sleeping with him or was to get his

account." He thought about Ashley's intense interest in Airways, her pursuit of him, all in the name of advertising. The pieces might fit to tell a nasty story about her. Well, he did not feel like bothering. Her ads were good and he had bought them, but he could drop her any time he wanted.

At nine, Porter Lamaretta called Mason. "Well, the clouds are lifting for you, Hank. Congratulations." Lamaretta sounded as though he had rocks in his throat. "I have the will here, and we may as well read it today. Your son is anxious to get to school and…"

"What about this morning?" Mason said.

"All right, if you like, fine."

In the next hour, Mason and his son were seated in front of Lamaretta's large, cluttered desk in a massive, oak-paneled office. Lamaretta kept shoving his black-rimmed glasses against his face. He reminded Mason of a whale propped up in his chair.

Hank turned around to look at Mary, who was seated behind Everett. Mary smiled at him, but Mason knew by her red eyes she had been crying.

"This is, of course, a lengthy will but the portions that concern the three of you, her family, are short," Lamaretta said.

Mason did not hear the long, legal passages Lamaretta spouted off. He was waiting for the portion of the will that refereed to his son.

"To my son, Everett, I leave the bulk of my estate, including my real estate, stock portfolio—with the exception of that left to my husband, Hank Mason—and the villas in France and Italy…" Porter went on, reading what seemed to Hank an endless list.

Mason looked at his son. "I'm happy about this, Everett." Mason put his hand on the boy's shoulder.

"And to my husband, Hank Mason, I bequeath what I know he will love best, the $3 million in stock I own in his airline, Airways International," Porter read on. He glanced at Mason for a reaction, Mason assumed.

So this was the irony in her will. It was a clever message, Mason thought. He could not remember Lenoir's being a major stock-holder so she must have bought the stock in the name of a company.

"You, Hank, become the executor of the estate. This is a big responsibility, and you are compensated financially for it, you understand," Lamaretta said. "You are to see that Mary is taken care of for the rest of her life."

Mason put an arm around Mary, and another on his son's shoulder, when Lamaretta finished the reading. "Well, it is all over now, really over," Mason said.

"I may be out later to see how you're putting the airline back together. Is that okay?" Everett said.

Mason stared at his son. "Yes, yes. I wish you would." Mason took Mary's hand. "I'll be seeing you, Mary. I promise you that. You'll be all right, won't you?"

"Of course, Mr. Mason. Mrs. Mason was very generous to me. I'll be at the house if you need me," she said, looking from Hank to Everett.

"And now I have a lot of work to do," Mason said. When he left them, Mason felt severed from the old ties and bonds and wounds. He could not ever remember feeling freer, and he hoped that Everett would find the same sensation.

Mason was back in his office by 11 that morning. He was unable to move from his phone. All the buttons were lighted up on his seven-line directory. There were good wishes from the board members, the Florida governor, the state's and U.S. Senators, employees, customers. It was Christmas, he thought, as he finally got up from his chair, his bad leg numb and pained after the long, busy morning. He told his secretary to assure everyone who called that he would return each call, but he had to get out from under at the moment.

"Here's one I think you must return now, Mr. Mason," his secretary said. She handed him a note and went back to the blinking lights on her phone directory.

Raising his shoulders in puzzlement, he read the words which said a lieutenant from the local police needed to talk with Mason at once. He returned to his office and dialed the number on the note. "What's happened?" he asked the officer.

"We've got a problem," the gruff voice answered. "It's Miss Bellam. Now your men and our men were on the case, and both of them followed her to a small grocery store this morning. They waited outside and she never came out. Now we've got the store closed, and we've searched it high and low. It looks like she's been abducted."

"Oh, God," Mason sighed. He sat down behind the table. What in hell's name were those idiots doing letting her go in there alone? "What can we do?"

"We're working on it. It's a kidnapping, maybe. We don't know. I've got a special detail on this case, Mr. Mason, because of all the trouble around Miss Bellam before. Her family's being covered, of course. Incoming calls are tapped. We'll let you know the minute we hear anything. It could be the same people that attacked her before. I've got the whole file out here, and we're questioning the union people."

"You know about the calls I got? The one that prompted me to get your protection this time for Trina?"

"That call could be related, but there's no way of telling. It could be anybody out there who called you. Or it could be all carefully plotted. We'll get back to you, Mr. Mason, whenever we have our first real lead."

"I feel like I'm the reason for this damn mess. If anything happens to her…"

"Mr. Mason, you're not the cause. Some damn low-lifes out there are to blame. We need your support now. So get hold of yourself and stand by."

Who was the policeman kidding? Of course there was a connection between the call and Trina's abduction. Of course it was all part of the same plan. It had to be. There was no telling what the monsters would do to her, short of killing her. Mason quivered inside and his hands shook.

When he called Trina's parents, her mother answered. Her voice was low and Mason knew she was crying. "We'll find her," Mason said. "Please have faith, Mrs. Bellam, that we will." As he spoke Mason felt a hollowness inside, knowing that he had no right to offer consolation. But if Mrs. Bellam was helped at all by his deception, then it served a purpose. The truth was, Mason admitted to himself, he was scared to death. The world seemed to tremble under his feet, and he knew that no matter how much he loved his airline, how relieved he was to see it come together again, he was more concerned about the safety of the girl to whom he had brought so much trouble.

Mrs. Bellam broke into sobs, and Mason told her he would be there at her house in minutes. Whitefield said he would handle Mason's load at the airline. "It's the worst time to run out on my own business, Whitefield, but I have to do it."

"I can't imagine what takes you away, Hank, not at a time like this. But go and don't worry about us."

"It's Trina, Whitefield. You'll read about it in the afternoon papers and hear about it on TV and radio. It's on now, probably. She's been kidnapped, abducted. Remember the threatening call? It wasn't idle talk."

"I can't believe it," Whitefield said.

"It's real, believe me. The police are staked out at her house, and we're waiting for some kind of ransom or word, at least."

When Mason reached the Bellam place, he saw a a fortress with police cars circled around the small house. One of the officers asked Mason for his ID the minute he arrived. The living room was crowded with men and women working on phones and electronic equipment. Some of the officers were flipping through scrapbooks of family photos. Nodding to a few of the people as he walked through the room, Mason made his way into the kitchen where he found Mrs. Bellam. Her back was arched over the table, and she was staring into a cup of coffee. She shook her head at Mason when he put a hand on her shoulder.

"The police have gotten a call from the abductor. They'll tell you all about it," she said. "They want a million dollars in cash by midnight tonight," Mrs. Bellam said.

"Who's in charge here, Mrs. Bellam?"

"Lieutenant Davidoff of the FBI. He's in the other room. I'll get him for you."

When Mrs. Bellam came back, Davidoff was with her. After shaking Mason's hand, he motioned for Mason to follow him outside.

"We've gotten the call we wanted. The abductors have demanded a million in cash and named Airways' president as the source of the money. We have directions from the parties—there were two voices on the line. We've got 'em recorded, and we want you to listen to them to see if you can recognize either as the male who called you about Miss Bellam. The problem now is getting the money to them."

"What do you mean?"

"Are you willing to put up that kind of money? I have to be honest. This has to be money. They might kill this young woman if we try any tricks."

"Of course I'm willing. How will we handle it?"

"You and I will contact your banks, and then a number of banks will work getting the cash together. It will be delivered by armored guard to us."

"What did these people say to you about Trina?"

"It's brutal, Mr. Mason. They said they'd butcher her. I don't think you want to hear the rest right now. You'll hear in time."

"You think this is connected with the union, the striking union?" Mason asked.

"Who knows?" the young man said, kicking at the grass with the toe of his shoe. "It's a crazy world. People are liable to do anything they tell you on the phone. It could be connected with one of your unhappy unions or union members. Maybe it's just a couple of members who didn't get what they wanted out of the settlement or didn't get big union jobs and somehow blame you. Maybe it's somebody who saw a chance to extort money."

"Should we start now on the money-raising plan?" Mason looked at the man's clear green eyes and straight blond hair. "And I want to go to deliver it."

"I'm afraid we can't risk that, Mr. Mason. We're sending a messenger."

"Risk it! My God, Davidoff, this girl means everything to me. I can't sit around while you do everything and I wait for the story."

"We respect you, Mr. Mason, and your wishes and your willingness to help. I'll do whatever I can to help you, but I can't promise anything. I take orders, you know."

"I'll talk to your superior and get his okay."

In the next two hours, Mason made arrangements with several South Florida banks to assemble the money which had to be a loan based on his own stock in the airline. His company could not part with that kind of money at the moment. He also listened to the tapes of the callers, and Mason thought he recognized one of them as the man who had threatened him by phone. When he finished those chores, Mason spoke to the FBI chief who game him permission, pending the signing of a waiver, to go with Davidoff and his team to deliver the money and pick up Trina.

When Mason got a minute to himself, he prayed. It was the first time in years he had asked for higher than human help. Struggling at first with the words, he felt them coming easier as he concentrated.

The Bellams left their house and went to stay with their minister. There they would tape TV messages aimed at appealing to the kidnappers or to anyone who knew anything about the kidnappers or Trina's whereabouts.

"This is a terrible thing to have happen just as your airline is going back to work," Davidoff said when the two men sat in the Bellam kitchen drinking coffee. "You're a very important man in this state and in the nation. I'd hate to see anything happen to you, Mr. Mason."

"I'd hate to see anything happen to Trina, Davidoff. And besides, we're all important. Human beings are important."

Excusing himself, Mason left the house and drove down to a drugstore on U.S. 1 where he picked up the *Miami Herald* and the *Palm Beach Post-Times*. Both of the papers carried the story of Trina's kidnapping in the front-page headlines. Airways' return to work was relegated to a one-column head at the bottom of both front pages.

He thumbed through the *Herald* to a full page ad announcing the end of the strike and Airways' New Sky service. So there it was, in the biggest, boldest type made—Ashley's new campaign. A picture of a mechanic, a stewardess, a pilot, a reservations agent— all bona fide Airways employees—waving from the wing of a DC-10. "We've made a new kind of sky for you. Come on up with us," the copy read. Mason liked it. Yes, it had class and a kind of reality that would appeal to business people and tourists.

He called Ashley at the office she had taken in his internal advertising department.

"I wondered if you'd call, Hank. Are you all right?"

"Why shouldn't I be all right?"

"After what happened in New York—I thought I'd never hear from you again. I don't know what I did, but I'm sorry for whatever it is or was..."

"Forget that. We can't live in the past. And it was my behavior that was wrong. Forget it."

"Who is this Trina Bellam I've been reading and hearing..."

"I like the campaign you've done, Ashley," he said, ignoring her question about Trina.

"Who is Trina Bellam?"

There was an insistence to Ashley's voice that Mason found

annoying. "You must know she is a stewardess. She was a union leader once."

"She must be special, hmm? The story is all over the office here—they've asked a million dollars and Airways is putting it all up."

"Is there anything else on your mind? You should be damn happy about this campaign of yours."

"I am happy. When are you coming back to the office?"

"I don't know. Tomorrow maybe."

"Well, I want to see you and so does your son. He's leaving for school and you should talk with him."

"I know that, Ashley. I did not plan what's happening. I'll see my son. We've had a talk."

"I hope it involved me…I've got to see you, Hank. Now. I can't wait till tomorrow."

"Ashley, you're out of your mind. I can't see you now or anybody else. You know what I'm involved in."

"Well, if you want your son and you want me to handle your ads right now, you'd better see me."

Mason sighed. "All right, Ashley. It's a ridiculous request but all right. It'll have to be near here…there's a place, a lounge on U.S. 1. It's Mike's—right side of the highway going north, right inside the Jupiter limits. I'll see you there in an hour. And I don't know why the hell I'm agreeing to this."

"You won't be sorry, Hank. You'll see."

Finding a booth at Mike's, which was empty except for himself, the bartender, and a lone drinker at the bar, Mason wondered what the hell he was doing here meeting Ashley when all his thoughts should be on Trina. Worse, Mason was on his second Scotch when Ashley finally slid into the booth seat opposite him.

"You look really down, and you have positives…" she said.

"Ashley, my God, you're inhuman. There's a girl, one of my stewardesses, kidnapped. She could be dead…"

"You've never been that concerned over a stewardess before."

"This has never happened to one of them before. There's no point to this interrogation, Ashley. Why did you have to see me?" Mason tried to quell his anger, but he wanted to tear out of this bar and leave Ashley. She was disgusting.

"More lives than you think are on the line now. Yours and mine and your son's. I want to know exactly where I stand and where he does."

"You're mixing apples and oranges, Ashley. This is no time…"

"Yes, it is, my darling."

"I'm sitting on a keg of dynamite right now."

"Okay, let's really blow off the lid. It's either this stewardess or me and your son. I'm the key, the only key to him right now."

"You're forcing me, Ashley. You want it straight? You'll get it straight. You've been fun. You're bright and beautiful and I like you. But it's over…it's just over. You won't drop my account. I could ruin you for that, Ashley, and you know it. My son, I'll have to deal with him myself. Don't threaten me with my own son."

"You think you're holding all the cards, then, don't you? Don't be so sure. There are ways I have of getting out of the responsibilities I have to Airways. And you really don't know what my relationship is with your son. And as far as Trina goes, do you think she'll even speak to you after what you've done to her life?"

She was bluffing on most of these questions—except the one about Trina. He was not sure of what Trina would do. "You have no damn business questioning Trina. She is none of your concern."

"You're a fool, Hank Mason. And so am I to have wasted my precious time. You may come back to me, though. Don't be certain of your course yet." Ashley gritted her teeth, and suddenly she was not the ravishing creature she once had been to him.

Ashley picked up her bag and slid her full cocktail glass across the table. The liquid spilled from the overturned glass and ran over the edge of the table and onto his lap.

"Get out of here in a hurry, Ashley!" Mason glared at her, trying to contain his rage. Damn her ass, he thought, when she had disappeared. Using his son to get to him. And pitting herself against a helpless girl whom he might never see again—alive. Mason found a phone booth in the rear of the bar and rang Everett at the Palm Beach house. Mary called his son to the phone.

Thank God he was home, Mason thought.

"Yes," the boy answered.

There were no negative tones in his voice, just an openness that Mason had hoped would be there. "Look, Ev, I'm going through hell right now with this kidnapping mess. The strike, the bombing, now this...I've been in a whirlwind, well, I wanted you to know that's why I haven't been in touch. What are your plans now?"

"I'm off to school in a couple of days."

"I see. Then your life is moving again...in a direction. You've got everything you need? I wish we had more time, Ev. Well, hell, I'll make the time. I've got to see you before you leave."

"There's no problem, I understand, Dad. I understand. There'll be time for us."

Mason paused. He wondered if his son was just appeasing him as some sort of punishment for neglecting him all these years. No, he could not afford that kind of distorted analysis now. He would have to accept Everett as he presented himself. "I'll sign off then, Ev. And thanks. I will make time."

Whether or not Mason was reading his son correctly, he felt more secure just having heard him. Ashley had succeeded at one thing— putting a scare into him, making him act on the bare thread of a relationship he had with Everett. Now he would have to begin to build some solid ground with his son. And he would. They might never be close, but at least they would talk to each other and share something of their lives.

Mason knew now that he did not want Ashley in any way. He saw her as she was, as she had always been. And he was beginning to get a picture of himself through her...he did not like what he saw of either of them.

✈

On his way back to the Bellam house, that sickening fear seized Mason again, and he wanted to strangle the men or women or both who had taken Trina into their hell.

When Mason arrived at the Bellams' home, it was dusk. The patrol cars were still parked around in the yard, and Davidoff stood by the front door, his arms folded. He nodded at Mason, who walked with his hands in his pockets up to the door. "What's the word?" Mason said.

"We've got our instructions all translated into logistics. Midnight tonight. And just you and a few of our staff in support of you are going on this mission. We'll only be going five miles away from here to a deserted area. We've got it all staked out."

"You're not planning to open fire."

"No," Davidoff said. "The enemy probably won't be going in till after dark, and we couldn't find them in the underbrush even with low-flying helicopters. No, we can't risk anything now. Wells Fargo will bring the money here to us, and we'll leave it, as we've been told to do, in a small house after 11. That's supposed to be in front of a bigger house where they have, or will have, Trina. When the money is passed through an opening in the door in that small shack, we wait 20 minutes and then walk to the big house. There we might find Trina unharmed.

"There should not be any gun play. We have every conceivable road watched. They could get away in a swamp buggy or by plane or chopper. We'll eventually get them; they're fools to hold her in a house in that kind of setting. But they are fools any way you look at them."

"You think this will work out all right?"

"I don't know. If they get nervous, they could blow the whole thing. You never know, Mr. Mason, with nuts like this. You just never know, and you don't dare take chances where there's a life at stake."

"You have any more leads about who these people are?"

"Our bureau says it does, but we'll have to see. Tonight is bound to produce some more tips."

Mason lighted a cigarette and stood silent for a while. What if this were just an act after the fact? What if Trina were dead now, and they were just waiting to collect the money?

"You want to change your mind about anything?" Davidoff asked.

"No, it's just the waiting I hate. If I seem nervous it's because I am. You had anything to eat, Davidoff?"

The agent shook his head no, and they headed for a nearby hamburger drive-in, using Davidoff's unmarked car. En route, the police radio voices that blurted out annoyed Mason. "You leave that thing on all the time, Davidoff?"

"Have to." Davidoff glanced over at Mason. "Just like you do in one of those big aircraft of yours. Come to think of it, I've always wanted to fly."

When they returned to the Bellam house, they found a smattering of policemen drinking coffee, smoking, and waiting. Radio equipment cluttered the front room, and Mason felt time running out. The urgency was pressing in on all of them. There were tense faces all around him.

Davidoff ran through the night's plan with Mason and two officers, who were armed with pistols strapped to their shoulders. They got into Davidoff's car, with Mason in front with the suitcases of money and Davidoff driving.

After a few miles, Davidoff pulled off the hard road and onto winding dirt ruts. The lights of the car showed them high, dry pine-tree land. Palmetto bushes stuck wide fronds out over the road and as the car passed them slowly, they bent, making scraping sounds against the metal. Mason could feel the wetness of the night. Dew had formed, and there was a fog floating in the headlights.

About half a mile beyond the turn-in, they saw a small wooden house. Its white paint was peeling off in blotches, and the only window they could see was broken, the remaining glass jagged and in high peaks. The lights of the car reflected in the pieces of glass.

The two officers in the back got out and went around the car and pushed the door of the house open. It creaked. Then they motioned Davidoff and Mason to come on. They left the car doors open and the engine running. Mason carried the cases of money. When he and Davidoff were inside the house, Davidoff turned on a flashlight to search for the door with the opening. When Davidoff found it, he walked with Mason and they shoved the luggage through the large, rectangular hole. Mason broke out in a heavy sweat which he cleared off his forehead with a handkerchief.

"Okay, let's get back to the car," Davidoff said finally.

The foursome waited in the car for the appointed 20 minutes. They all smoked, and they did not speak as they watched the small house for any sign of motion.

"Okay, we'll head for the main house now," Davidoff said finally.

Mason could not remember being more terrified as he followed Davidoff. In search of the bigger house, the pair made their way through the thicket of leafy vines and ferns. Their companions followed.

"It should be about 50 feet," Davidoff whispered.

They were still in the beam of headlights from the car.

"There is it, Mason," Davidoff said.

It was an old barn structure with two stories, a sagging front porch and broken square pillars. From upstairs came a light from a single bulb suspended from the ceiling. Strange, Mason thought, that there should be electricity in this deserted house. Someone must be staying here or someone stayed here and left. Well, what the hell did any of that matter now? Was Trina in there?

Mason felt his heart pound against the wall of his chest as he held his hand on his shirt. The pair walked into the house where downstairs there was complete darkness. Davidoff found their way with the flashlight and led them to the stairs.

"You all right, Mr. Mason?" Davidoff asked.

"Sure, go on, Davidoff, I'm fine."

The stairs swayed under their feet, the banister bending as they pulled at it for support. Atop the stairs a shaft of light shone on a dirty, rotted wood floor. They walked to the doorway where the light came from and went in. There was a long wooden table, crudely made from junk lumber. On it was a white envelope under a large rock, with Mason's name scribbled across the front. Davidoff handed it to Mason.

"This is just another stall, Mr. Mason. Open it." Inside there was a note written in pencil. It was signed "Trina."

> *Dear Hank,*
>
> *I am alive and they will tell you where I am tomorrow morning. They will call your office. Please do as they say. I will be all right…if there is no shooting after this note is found.*

"I'll be damned." Mason said.

"At least we didn't find her dead. This just assures the culprits a safe way out of here with the money."

"And what about Trina?" Mason asked, his hand rubbing the back of his neck which ached from the strain of the night.

"I don't know about Miss Bellam. I don't know. Now we go back to the Bellam house and wait. Come on."

Mason was numb as he walked back to the car with Davidoff and the other two men who had covered the house while Mason and Davidoff were inside.

Davidoff ground the car along the ruts again and onto the hard road, and Mason felt empty and useless. The mission was nothing but a heist, a robbery.

"This is really not far from what I expected, Mr. Mason. They were too smart to be around there and too smart to leave any traces of the girl. They'll get the money now. We have the property covered but we can't fire, only track them."

"What makes you think they'll let her live? She knows who these people are now."

"They'll have a new scheme for us in the morning," Davidoff answered.

"Why should they call? They have the money."

"They're greedy. They want more."

"God, will this never end?" Mason's voice was weary and disgusted.

"Nightmares end, Mr. Mason. They all end sometime."

"So I wait at the office until I get the call."

"Look, these people are smart, but they're stupid overall. They're not wise enough to quit now. That's our only hope—that greed will keep driving them on."

"You don't believe they'd take another risk for more money."

"Sure. Chances are they're planning to leave the country, cross over a border somewhere, get a small boat to carry them to a ship, anything."

Tears welled in Mason's eyes. He could not accept the possibility that Trina was dead. She had to be alive. Somewhere.

At the Bellam house, cars were parked everywhere. Floodlights from the house showed TV and radio station insignia on some of the cars. Groups of men and women in the yard pressed in as Davidoff and his party made their way up to the front door. They were stopped by reporters with microphones. Cameramen moved in on them, and the bright lights flooded out Mason's vision.

With swimming-like motions, Mason cut through the swell of people shaking his head and mumbling, "No comment," to the questions shot at him.

Uniformed policemen opened the door for Mason and Davidoff, and the two officers who had been through the ordeal with them stayed outside.

"There's no need to tell the press anything now, Mr. Mason. We'll handle all comments, and that's what our friends are telling them now. They'll badger you to death, but I suppose you know all about the press. They're just doing their job, I guess, but it's annoying to me sometimes. I suggest you leave by the back door, and I'll have one of my men drive you home.

"Fine," Mason said. His face was drawn, the lines across his forehead and around his mouth deeply etched into his skin. At this moment, he felt like getting drunk.

Once back at The Breakers, he poured himself a small water glass of Scotch and drank it down in one swallow. Afterwards, he took a cold shower, dressed, and headed for his office. Retracing the night behind him, Mason could not believe any of it. He wondered now if he would ever see Trina again.

Chapter 16

At sunrise the next morning, Mason paced the floor of his office and glanced at the phone every other minute. More than anything in the world, he wanted to hear the voice that had threatened him. Hearing it would give him a thread of hope of seeing Trina again.

When the phone did ring, it jolted Mason, and he had to force himself to answer it.

"You don't usually let your phone ring that long, Mason. What's wrong?" Whitefield asked from the other end.

"Well, it's just that I was expecting someone..." He ran his hand over his chin, pensively. "Is everything okay with you?"

"I should ask you that. I heard about last night. They got the money but didn't deliver Trina. I'll come to your office. We'll talk."

Whitefield sat on the sofa, studying Mason's face. Mason fidgeted with his hands and tried to walk his worry down.

"You're awaiting some word. But you're not sure she's alive, are you?" Whitefield's voice was solemn.

"I guess we're just stupid—the police, the FBI, me—to think there's hope. They've won. Everything's over."

"You never know in these cases, Hank. You're dealing with insanity of a kind and you cannot predict..."

"It's as though it's some horrible, monstrous force out there that I never really knew existed. I'm not paranoid, Whitefield, never have been—until now anyway."

"Then take it easy. This is another ordeal we just have to wait out."

"You see, *if* she's dead, I killed her. I've brought everybody suffering lately. Seems it's all crashing around me and the people I care about."

"You're not a man to give up, Hank. Let's not assume anything about Trina. Not yet. You've got to hold on, Hank. And you will. I know you will."

Mason paced back and forth, half aware that Whitefield was there with him, half watching the phone, and cursing himself inside. If only this had happened to him instead of Trina. Life never worked out fairly for anybody.

He paused, thinking that when he was riding high he never viewed life that way. Until the strike, until his wife's death, until he met Trina, he had never really taken stock of his life. Now he had to—if he was to go on in any sensible way. Deep within himself, he felt a kind of rebirth coming, as if a new person was about to emerge. It was an overpowering sensation and he did not know if he could handle it. He was standing on the edge, but this time it was not fear that gripped him but an overwhelming urge to try to act out of compassion for himself and everybody else.

Whitefield cleared his throat. "You don't need me here with you, Hank. I should get back to my office. I hope…well, you know what I hope and pray for."

Mason shook his head and Whitefield left him. For a minute Mason tried to get interested in the stacks of paperwork before him. The sentences in the letters he was to sign made no sense to him. He could not concentrate enough to read. How could he pay attention to anything now except the phone, his only link to Trina's destiny.

It is strange, he reflected, that at a time like this you begin to summarize your life, evaluate it, and question it. He had never taken a long look at Hank Mason, but there was that absolute demand at this minute that he reach for that insight.

When his phone rang, Mason raced to pick it up. "Yes," there was an urgency in his voice. "Yes, you say you heard her voice, Davidoff? It wasn't a recording. She's in San Diego. What the hell… but she's alive? Another trap. Is this another trap? Let's hope, let's pray it's not. I'll get there right away. The next flight west."

Mason could not believe what he had heard. Trina was alive and with the FBI in California. Davidoff had talked to the police, his colleagues, and Trina herself. Her abductors flew with her to

California the night before, let her go in San Diego, and fled over the border to Mexico. The kidnappers were not union members but a handful of young men who told Trina they needed the money for a cause they did not define, Davidoff said. But Mason could find out all the details himself—he could call Trina now.

"No, no calls—that's not good enough. Just let her know I'm on my way." Mason heard his voice rising. The excitement of this good news was almost too much to process.

In the minutes that followed, Mason operated in a haze of happiness and shock. His emotions wavered. He still could not grasp that she was there waiting to come home.

Mason ran to the door of his office and told his secretary he would be leaving immediately for the West Coast. There was a flight with one stop in New Orleans, and it would leave in 15 minutes. Mason raced for the crew bus downstairs and told the driver to get him onto the field and to the DC-10 that was loading now.

As he boarded, a stewardess asked to see his ticket before he had a chance to pull out his ID. She blushed and smiled when he handed his identification to her.

"It's all right. Everyone who works for Airways doesn't know me by sight," he told the girl.

Mason took a rear seat in the tourist section, breathing deeply when he began to realize the nightmare was ending. In four hours he would be with Trina. No, he could not wait to hear her voice. He would call her at the number Davidoff gave him when the plane stopped in New Orleans.

After the aircraft lifted off, took its swing over the long stretch of beach, and headed due west out over the aqua-blue water, Mason closed his eyes. He felt alone with himself for the first time in many months. But this feeling was different. There was a peace of mind attached to it. He could stop running for a while and look at his life and find out where he was going...or could he?

In a way he was living out a dream, but if he turned the coin he was also facing a terrible reality. What if Trina did not want to see him? What if this experience had embittered her to the point of hating him? Why was he running to her with a confidence she really had not inspired?

He had no right to expect anything from Trina. After all, how did she know that he was beginning to change his perspective, his values? Magically, he had been given a second chance in life. He knew now what his mistakes were; he even knew what love was. Lenoir had taught him, by wasting her life because she cried out for nothing more than his love. Love between a father and child. His son represented the possibility of that love. He had failed Lenoir completely, but he would not lose his son. And now there was an opportunity with Trina—if he had not destroyed his chances already. He could offer Trina a full life, the material things, and love. He would not return to that charade of a man he had played before. Visions of that Hank Mason ran through his head, and memories of what that creature had done to himself and to others made him ashamed. He reminded himself that if he did regress to the Ashleys of his life, then a decent life for him in the future would be impossible. A double life, criss-crossing when he felt the urge, would never work. No, he was committed to a new start, and he would have to prove that to himself and Trina. He knew she liked him, but could she love him? They would need so much time. They had had so little before...

When the plane landed in New Orleans, Mason did not get off but rose and stretched, and got a cup of water from one of the galleys. If he called her and she told him not to come to her, then what? It was an option he was not leaving open for her or for himself. He had to face her, to know what her reaction was today—and by that response he would know if there was anything in the future for them.

In the air again, he asked himself why he was laying his whole life out on the line like this, and he answered himself quickly, the speed of his answer convincing him he was on the right track. He simply could not survive as that selfish bastard he had been. How long can you go on treating people as if they were plastic, blaming them for their frailties and allowing your own, denying them any real human warmth and robbing them of their emotions? Ironically, when you hurt others, you hurt yourself most, he thought.

And worst of all, he realized, you are not free when you are bound up in satisfying your flesh desires. When you are lost in the concern for other people, as he had been with the FBI trying to find Trina, only then can you join hands with humanity and move outside yourself to a world of new feelings, good feelings.

When the passengers around him began to disembark, Mason sat still for a few minutes until a stewardess handed him a note from the captain. The FBI and party were inside the terminal waiting for Mason. His hands began to shake. "Thank you," he told the stewardess. Trina, then, was here at the airport, waiting to catch a flight home.

As Mason walked through the terminal, he spotted a group of men and a girl in the distance, standing at one side of the Airways ticket counter. Everyone in his view disappeared when Mason realized the girl was Trina.

Her legs moved slowly at first, and then they broke into a fast walk—and then into a run. Mason felt his body rise, soar off the ground in rhythm to hers. The yards between them seemed miles. She was closer now and there were tears—no, smiles—as her arms reached out to him. He tasted the salt of his own tears as their hands clasped and their bodies touched.

www.ingramcontent.com/pod-product-compliance
Lightning Source LLC
Chambersburg PA
CBHW071912220626
47052CB00002B/312